THE HIDDEN SHRINE OF TMOCANOTZ

Author: Tom Knauss
Project Managers: Zach Glazar and Tom Knauss
Editor: Jeff Harkness
Art Direction: Casey Christofferson
Layout and Graphic Design: Charles A. Wright
Cover Design: Charles A. Wright
Cover Art: Adrian Landeros
Interior Art: Julio de Carvalho
Cartography: Robert Altbauer
Fantasy Grounds Conversion: Michael G. Potter

FROG GOD GAMES IS:

Bill Webb, Matthew J. Finch, Zach Glazar, Charles A. Wright, Edwin Nagy, Mike Badolato, John Barnhouse

ADVENTURES
WORTH
WINNING

FROG GOD GAMES

ISBN: 978-1-6656-0136-8

TABLE OF CONTENTS

THE HIDDEN SHRINE OF TMOCANOTZ

"INSANITY HAS NO MASTER."

— AN AZTLI PROVERB

The Hidden Shrine of Tmocanotz is an adventure for four upper Tier 1 characters that introduces them to an old foe making an appearance in the forsaken Izmalli Swamp on the island of Tehuatl. In a subterranean and partially submerged complex beneath the ground, the deranged worshippers of a foul deity have made a sudden and unexpected resurgence in their efforts to spread madness and wickedness beyond their isolated corner of the wetlands.

ADVENTURE BACKGROUND

Long ago, the cipatenhuas migrated to Tehuatl from a distant land. The great sea serpent Cipactli led his minions across Mother Oceanus in their quest to find a new home. When the beast and the crocodilian humanoids under his protection reached the island's shore, their arrival had been expected. The devious god Itztliteotl awaited Cipactli and his followers. The consummate trickster had longed for this opportunity to have some fun at the fearsome yet dimwitted monster's expense, yet in this case, the joke was on him. Unwilling to play the cunning deity's game, Cipactli opened his mighty jaws and clamped down on Itztliteotl's foot, tearing the appendage from the outraged hero-god's leg. In a fit of rage, Itztliteotl slew the mighty beast and hurled his lifeless body back into the sea.

The startled cipatenhuas who followed Cipactli to their new homeland nervously awaited the angry deity's vengeance. But despite their leader's transgression, the Smoking Mirror spared their lives though not without a price. Because they came from the water, he cursed the cipatenhua race, condemning them to never set foot on dry land lest they suffer his wrath. Grateful for his mercy, the reptilian cipatenhuas paradoxically paid homage to the jaguar lord who took pity on their people after exacting his spiteful revenge upon them and their descendants. Confined to the aquatic swamps and marshes along the island's eastern shore, the migrants undertook the arduous task of rebuilding their communities and adapting to a fresh start in a distant land under the aegis of a foreign god and his worshippers, the Aztlis, the island's indigenous humans.

Over the next 1,000 years, the cipatenhuas gradually adjusted to their new lives in Tehuatl. They forged friendly relationships with some of their fellow humanoids while engaging in protracted battles against aggressive adversaries who threatened their territory. Despite their inability to leave the wetlands, many of their race embraced the sly Itztliteotl as their divine benefactor, yet a small minority chafed at the notion of venerating the wily being who condemned them to a miserable existence in the island's stinking wetlands. Unwilling to accept another god indigenous to the island, they turned to a fellow import — the deranged Frog God Tsathogga. Although they expressed some trepidation venerating a deity with no comprehensible agenda other than sowing murder and mayhem, the crazed demon prince seemed to be the best choice in an imperfect world.

One year ago, a small enclave of Tsathogga's cipatenhua worshippers broke away from their community and founded a hidden shrine to their vile god in a catacomb of tunnels and chambers beneath a small pond where they could clandestinely perform their sinister rites. To complete this undertaking, this small band of worshippers led by Griigg the frog prince began kidnapping other humanoids to serve as victims for their sacrificial rites and slaves to perform menial tasks within the shrine. With their power steadily growing, Griigg and his followers now seek to expand their influence and that of their insane benefactor within their isolated section of the Izmalli Swamp.

ADVENTURE SYNOPSIS

The adventure begins with Tsathogga's cipatenhua worshippers venturing outside the secure confines of their underwater complex in a search for fresh victims to sacrifice to their deranged deity or a new batch of slaves to mercilessly toil under their oppressive yoke. The characters may encounter the cipatenhuas during their hunt or they may become embroiled in the adventure's events after being asked to investigate the disappearance of someone who fell prey to the cipatenhuas. The characters may use their tracking ability to retrace the cipatenhuas' steps back to the edge of a pond that houses their subterranean shrine or the characters may discover the shrine's location through other means such as divination spells, information from a cipatenhua still loyal to Itztliteotl, or a captured cipatenhua follower of Tsathogga.

After locating the hidden entrance to the shrine, the characters must access the partially submerged complex through a tunnel filled with murky water. Here, the characters are free to explore the shrine, which includes living quarters for the cipatenhua residents, slave quarters, and food production and distribution areas, and the shrine's inner sanctum. The cunning cipatenhuas incorporated natural and manmade traps into their stronghold to deter intruders and also burrow into the earth searching for precious gemstones. When the characters bypass the shrine's cipatenhua and monstrous guards, they can reach the unholy shrine proper where the characters confront Griigg the frog prince and his demented minions.

STARTING THE ADVENTURE

The characters may start the adventure in one of the Izmalli Swamp's neighboring villages or while traveling to another location within the wetland from somewhere else. If the characters hail from the region, you may have a concerned family member approach the characters and ask them to search for a missing loved one. Alternatively, a religious, political, or economic interest may also solicit assistance from the characters to investigate a disappearance, strange event, or disruption to commercial traffic. For characters also partaking in the adventure ***The Re-education of Coyotl***, the town of Teohuacan detailed in that adventure provides a good starting point for the adventurers to begin their quest. Otherwise, you are free to use one of the communities from the ***Tehuatl*** sourcebook from **Frog God Games** as the characters' home base or you may create another small settlement of your choosing in any setting of your choice. If the characters are not local to the area, they could intervene in the middle of an attempted abduction or fall prey to a cipatenhua ambush while traveling through the area.

ADVENTURE HOOKS

You may use any of the following adventure hooks to immerse the characters into the story or invent one of your own depending upon how and where you want to start the adventure.

ABDUCTION

While traveling through a comparatively dry portion of the Izmalli Swamp, a character who succeeds on a DC 5 Wisdom (Perception) check hears a commotion coming from the brush ahead. Three Aztli teenagers (LN male human Aztli **tribal warriors**) struggle to fend off 6 **cipatenhuas** (see **Appendix A: New Monsters**) who accosted them while venturing through the wilderness. The humans appear badly injured, reduced to half their maximum hit points or fewer, while the cipatenhuas appear virtually unscathed, reduced 1d4 points below their maximum hit points. The humanoids seek to capture rather than kill the adolescents to use them as sacrifices to their profane deity Tsathogga. Alternatively, you may forego the adolescents altogether and instead have the cipatenhuas attempt to ambush the characters. In this case, the concealed cipatenhuas have advantage on their Dexterity (Stealth) checks contested by the characters' passive Perception. If the characters fail to notice the crocodilian humanoids hiding in the vegetation, the monsters surprise them. Adventurers who defeat the monsters may intensely question them, using Charisma (Intimidation or Persuasion) checks contested by the cipatenhuas' Wisdom (Insight) checks to learn of their intentions, the location of their shrine, and their allegiance to the Frog God Tsathogga. Otherwise, the characters can retrace their steps back to their shrine. The route crosses 1d4 streams along the way. At each crossing, a character must succeed on a DC 10 Wisdom (Survival) check to stay on the path.

BIG FISH

Two days ago, Tlacamichi, a local fisherman, told his wife and children that he was going into the swamp to his secret fishing hole and would be home before dusk that evening for dinner. He never came back. Naturally, his wife Tecaltin (CG female human Aztli **commoner**) fears for her husband's safety. She swears he would never abandon his family and has tirelessly prayed to Atoyatl to protect him. The distraught spouse implores the characters to find her husband and discover the truth about what happened to him. Tecaltin can provide no specifics regarding the secret fishing hole's precise spot, but believes she knows its general vicinity. She says he primarily caught catfish in what he described as a murky pond a short walk from the riverbank. She cannot pay the character for their services. Instead, Tecaltin frantically begs the adventurers to help her family, who are close friends with some influential people in town.

HERETICS

Itztliteotl's human representative in town, Huitayo (CN male human Aztli **priest**), greatly fears some of his cipatenhua followers whom he visits from time to time have gone astray from their faith and embraced a heretical new god in a vile shrine hidden somewhere in the wilderness. His most loyal acolyte Tzamma (use the **cipatenhua** stat block found in **Appendix A: New Monsters**) has heard some of his people speak of abandoning the Aztli deity and shifting their devotion to a foul new entity whose followers meet in a subterranean shrine somewhere in the wilderness. Tzamma has no knowledge of the gathering place's exact location, though he believes he knows the general area where it can be found. He agrees to take the characters there to find it and root out the evil within the unholy sanctum.

RUMORS

Numerous stories of dubious validity circulate among the populace in the region. The characters may overhear these tales being spread in a public setting or learn of them during a conversation with a local inhabitant. Likewise, the characters may have already gained some information about the area and its people through their personal experiences and education. Characters from the Izmalli Swamp have advantage on Intelligence (History and Religion) checks to recall details and information germane to current events in the region. A character who succeeds on a Charisma check may also hear more generalized gossip from third-party sources if the character can effectively communicate with the individual and the person has some knowledge of the area.

A character who succeeds on a DC 10 Intelligence (History or Religion) check (player's choice) as noted below remembers something about this topic that pertains to the current situation. Likewise, a character who succeeds on a DC 15 Charisma check while meeting the preceding conditions may also discover any of the following facts about the area. A successful check in one of the preceding fields does not grant access to every rumor. The parenthesis at the end of each rumor indicates the applicable area of expertise required to recall the information and whether the rumor is true or not.

TABLE 1–1: RUMORS

1d8	Rumor
1	The cipatenhuas are a race of crocodilian humanoids who arrived in Tehuatl roughly 1,000 years ago. They predominately dwell in the island's marshes and swamps. Although not overly aggressive, the cipatenhuas vigorously defend their territory. (Intelligence, History, or Charisma; this rumor is true)
2	When the cipatenhuas first arrived in Tehuatl, the Aztli god Itztliteotl cursed them because the giant beast leading them to the island bit off the angry deity's foot. For this reason, the cipatenhuas must always keep at least one foot wet at all times or suffer his wrath. Nonetheless, they primarily worship Itztliteotl though some sects have strayed from the faith over the years. (Intelligence, Religion, or Charisma; this rumor is true)
3	The cipatenhuas have an affinity for crocodiles, though some of them can supposedly transform into other reptiles or amphibians. (Intelligence, History, Religion, or Charisma; this rumor is true)
4	Frog people also inhabit the swamp and have been seen in greater numbers over the past several weeks. They seem to be intently searching for something. (Charisma; this rumor is true)
5	The gnolls from the neighboring grasslands recruited numerous spies throughout the swamp. An invasion may be imminent. (Charisma; this rumor is false)
6	Someone is raising the dead in the swamp! Bloated, waterlogged corpses are rising from the ground, seeking to feast on the flesh of the living. (Charisma; some undead are in the swamp, so this rumor is partly true though no one is actively raising them)
7	If you're inclined to dance, Org, the oafish troll who lives along the river will join you for a song or two. He is friendly with the local teenagers. (Charisma; this rumor is true)
8	A druid conducts bizarre experiments on the swamp's flora and fauna. Some of his abominations haunt the flooded forest (Intelligence, History, or Charisma; this rumor is false)

A character who succeeds on a DC 15 Intelligence (History or Religion) check (player's choice) as noted below remembers something about this topic that pertains to the current situation. Likewise, a character who succeeds on a DC 20 Charisma check while meeting the preceding conditions may also discover any of the following facts about the area. A successful check in one of the preceding fields does not grant access to every rumor. The parenthesis at the end of each rumor indicates the applicable area of expertise required to recall the information and whether the rumor is true or not.

TABLE 1–2: ADVANCED RUMORS

1d6	Rumor
1	A small yet bloodthirsty cult has arisen among the cipatenhuas. They purportedly worship a deity imported from a foreign land. Some even believe they established a shrine within the swamp. (Charisma; this rumor is true)
2	The cipatenhuas who venerate this god sacrifice living creatures to it. (Charisma; this rumor is true)
3	A band of warriors swear they saw a small, canine-like humanoid accompanying a cipatenhua in the swamp several days ago. (Charisma; this rumor is true)
4	Beware the cottage along the river. It is haunted. (Charisma; this rumor is partially true and refers to Eltezcatl's house, which is dangerous but not haunted)
5	Smugglers transporting illicit goods frequent the river and bury some of their wares beneath the mud for safekeeping. (Charisma; this rumor is mostly false)
6	The boggards are poised to attack the region. (Charisma; this rumor is false)

EVENTS

The following vignettes do not play an essential role in the adventure. Instead, they are intended to be interspersed into the story to give the characters additional clues and information in a nonconfrontational setting.

TABLE 1–3: ADVENTURE EVENTS

1d10	Event
1–3	Culalli, Itaca, Nenatl, Yaniyah, Yatzli, and Yotli (N female human Aztli **commoners**), six local teenage girls, infectiously giggle while performing a strange dance containing funny movements and silly lyrics. They beg the characters to join them and offer to teach them the odd steps. If the characters refuse to participate, the girls poke fun at them, telling the characters that even the troll by the river has more rhythm and dances alongside them. The girls' reference pertains to the encounter with **Org** detailed in Part One of the adventure.
4–5	Catuma (NG male human Aztli **commoner**), a local fisherman, has two large catfish in a net slung over his back. He claims the fish are so big that he and his family will be able to eat only one before the other spoils. He offers to sell the other catfish to the characters for the fair price of 2 cacao beans. If asked where he caught the fish, he provides general directions to a pond that is close to Tlacamichi's secret fishing hole from the preceding **Big Fish** adventure hook.
6–7	Two mid-sized hairless pet dogs (**mastiffs**) stand nose to nose and growl at each other while intently staring at a bone on the ground. The animals trade turns trying to grab the bone before being intimidated out of doing so by their canine counterpart. A character who looks at the bone without closely examining it and succeeds on a DC 20 Intelligence (Nature) check verifies it is not human, though it appears to be part of a flipper from a large aquatic mammal. Someone bold enough to grab the bone from the snarling dogs and closely study it has advantage on the preceding check.
8–9	Three teenage boys named Izmalla, Nematzo, and Tetzuo (CN male human Aztli **commoners**) are playing with a ball in an open field. The rambunctious boy converse about an alluring woman they saw walking in the swamp alongside her pet cat. They had never seen her before, but strangely each of their descriptions of the woman are different, yet the cat remains the same. Their discussion centers on the upcoming encounter **The Cat in the Hag's Hat**.
10	Itzlacoytl (LE male human **commoner**) drank more pulque than humanly possible. He lies on his side snoring loudly as some frothy liquid rolls down the side of his cheek. In his drunken stupor, he periodically blurts out statements about demons coming to get him. If roused from his slumber, the cantankerous old man profusely swears and tells the characters he knows nothing about demons and demands they let him sleep off his dreadful hangover.

PART ONE: THE IZMALLI SWAMP

Ominous, foreboding, disgusting, sweltering, and sticky are just some of the adjectives people use to describe these wetlands. From an ecological standpoint, the Izmalli Swamp is a semitropical saltwater swamp where roughly half the terrain lies submerged beneath at least several inches of standing water. Ponds, brooks, streams, and small rivers crisscross the soggy landscape with frequent regularity. The stifling heat and humidity wilt even the hardiest creatures within minutes, while iron and steel almost instantly start to rust when exposed to these warm, humid conditions. There are no formal roads or trails anywhere, though the lack of vegetation and slightly drier ground in some areas function as rudimentary paths cutting through the largely untamed wilderness. With the exception of these crude roadways, the balance of the swamp is treated as difficult terrain.

Local inhabitants rarely stray off the beaten path despite the increased likelihood of stumbling into an ambush, a booby trap, or a wild animal making its way through the swamp. Despite the dangers, expeditiousness and the fear of getting hopelessly lost in the uncharted wilderness play an important role in keeping most people from wandering off on their own in the wetlands. For every hour spent trekking through the Izmalli Swamp, there is a 25% chance of encountering one of the creatures appearing on **Table 1–4: Izmalli Swamp Wilderness Random Encounters**. If the characters exclusively remain on the path, the chance increases to 35%, but they encounter only humanoids or monsters. A rendezvous with an animal or monster is rerolled until the adventurers run into a humanoid or monster.

TABLE 1–4: IZMALLI SWAMP WILDERNESS RANDOM ENCOUNTERS

1d8	Encounter
1	1d2 + 1 cipatenhuas plus 1 cipatenhua disciple
2	1d3 + 3 crocodiles
3	1d2 + 1 giant toads
4	1d3 mudbog oozes
5	2 ogres
6	2 sloth vipers
7	1d4 + 3 tsathars
8	1d3 will-o'-wisps

CIPATENHUAS

The 1d2 + 1 **cipatenhuas** and their **cipatenhua disciple** (see **Appendix A: New Monsters** for both) routinely patrol the area around their shrine as they search for trespassers, fresh prey, and potential slaves. The crocodilian humanoids likely assess the adventurers as falling into the first category if they appear heavily armed and well-equipped. The cipatenhua disciple functions as the group's de facto leader and prefers to use his repertoire of spells and cantrips to snipe at the characters from afar while the cipatenhuas function as frontline troops. In this endeavor, the disciple may attempt to climb a nearby tree using his *spider climb* spell or potentially swim into the middle of a pond or stream and attack from that relatively safe location. Like the cipatenhuas in the preceding **Abduction** adventure hook, the characters can question these creatures to discover the shrine's location or follow their tracks back to the site.

Treasure: Each of the cipatenhuas carries a pouch containing 2d6 seashells worth 1 gp each. The disciple carries a pouch containing six moss agates worth 10 gp each.

CROCODILES

These hungry beasts predominately stick to the waterways and riverbanks in search of prey rather than walk along wet earth or even dry land for their next meal. When the characters encounter the reptiles, they are best suited for a fight in a shallow body of water rather than out in the open. The 1d3 + 3 **crocodiles** never fight as a cohesive unit and simply attack the nearest creature with unbridled ferocity. Despite their aggressiveness, the crocodiles are unwilling to risk their lives for a bite to eat. Each crocodile individually retreats back to the water if reduced to fewer than one-half its maximum hit points.

GIANT TOADS

Despite the amphibians' affiliation with the vile Frog God, these large beasts are not associated with the shrine in any way. Like the crocodiles, these creatures are best suited for an encounter within or along the edges of a body of water where they can leap onto their prey and bite their opponent before attempting to swallow them. The 1d2 + 1 **giant toads** fight as individuals rather than part of a coordinated team. Motivated predominately by hunger rather than aggression, a giant toad slinks back into the water and flees if an enemy escapes its belly or if it is unable to bite or swallow an opponent after three rounds of combat.

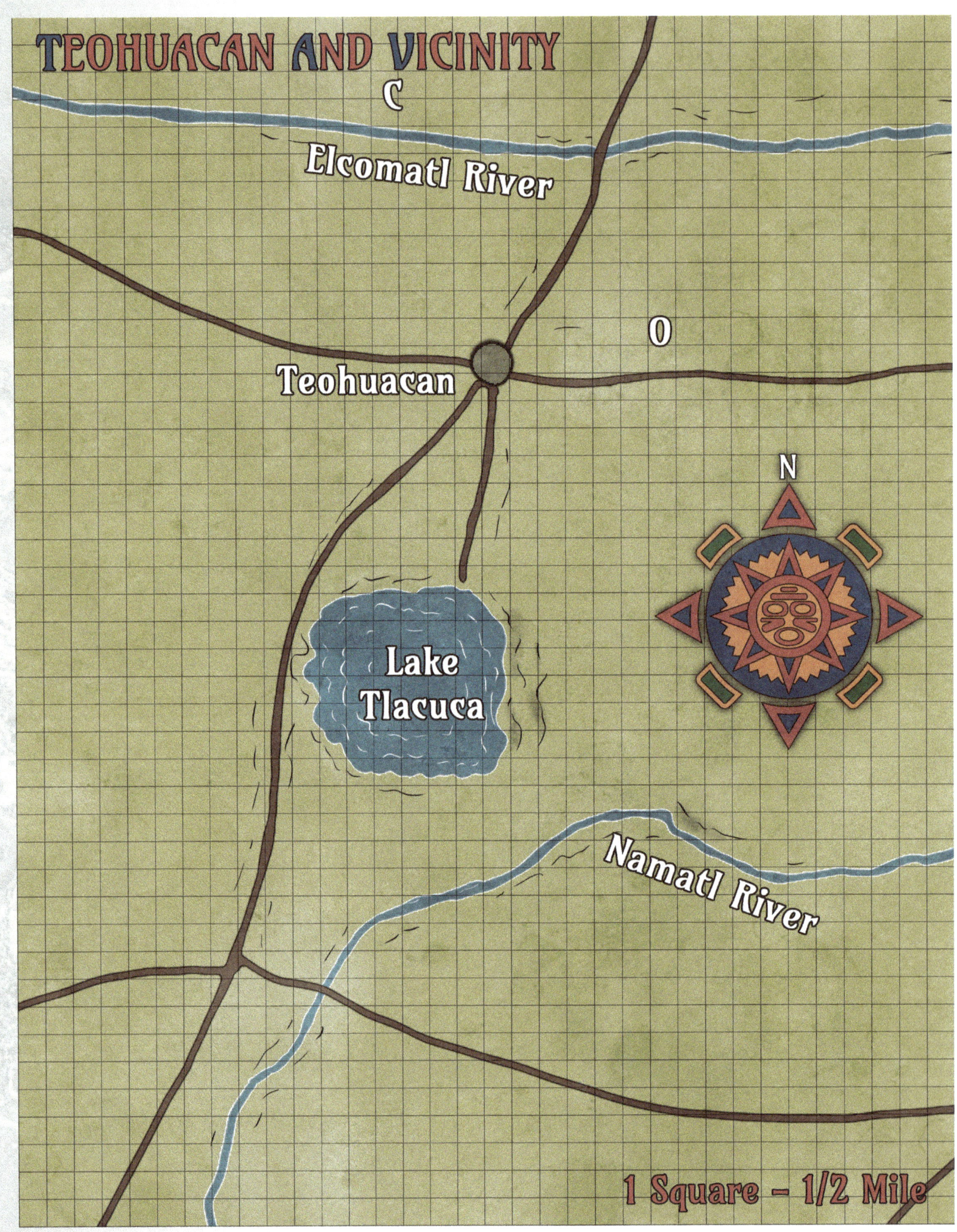

TEOHUACAN AND VICINITY
C
Elcomatl River
O
Teohuacan
N
Lake
Tlacuca
Namatl River
1 Square – 1/2 Mile

Mudbog Ooze

Murky pools of water are practically everywhere in the Izmalli Swamp, making it impossible to distinguish these mindless, amorphous blobs of protoplasm from the ordinary muddy pools strewn across the characters' path. Because of their ability to blend into their surroundings, the oozes stretch across the crude trails cut through the vegetation. When a creature steps on one of them or moves within 10 feet of it, the ooze attempts to engulf its victim and haul it into a neighboring body of water in an attempt to drown it and prevent rescuers from coming to the captured creature's aid. The 1d3 **mudbog oozes** (see **Appendix A: New Monsters**) have no concept of death so they continue fighting until slain.

Ogres

Tehuatl's small population of ogres generally dwell within the Tepepan Mountains, especially in the town of Hrawrg, otherwise known as Ogretown. However, these 2 **ogres** ventured from the comparatively safe confines of their mountainous home into the foul Izmalli Swamp on their way to meet with a fellow giant, Org, the river troll (see the upcoming **Org** encounter for more details), to gather intelligence about humanoid and monstrous activities within the Izmalli Swamp. The ogres, Grong and Hrang, follow a crude, hand-drawn map detailing how to navigate a path to Org's lair using local landmarks as guides. The oafish brutes cannot willingly pass up on opportunity to attack and bully humanoids smaller than themselves during the course of their mission. Their taste for flesh compels them to mercilessly assault elves, dwarves, and halflings whom they consider a delicacy. Fearful of failing Ogretown's masters, the giants propose a truce with the characters if seriously threatened and offer to take them to Org who may have some knowledge about the cipatenhuas' hidden shrine. If the characters accept the ogres' terms, the giants fulfill their end of the bargain by escorting them to Org's hideaway, though the treacherous ogres once again assault the characters if an opportunity presents itself once they reach their destination. Grong and Hrang know nothing about the Izmalli Swamp outside of their mission to rendezvous with the river troll.

Treasure: Each ogre carries a sack containing 3d6 gp. Grong also has a *spell scroll* (*bless*) that he looted from a dwarven cleric he killed in the mountains before the pair began their journey here.

Sloth Vipers

This mated pair of serpents loiters along the banks of a stream, brook, or river where they hid their nest containing three eggs within a dense thicket of vegetation. It takes a successful DC 15 Wisdom (Perception) check to spot these emerald-colored eggs amid the cluster of twisted vines, leaves, and dirt. Likewise, the ambush predator serpents also conceal their position within the trees. Because they have had ample time to create an ideal hiding space, the sloth vipers have advantage on their Stealth checks when the characters approach their lair. The snakes may either drop down on their intended target and bite it, or snap down on a victim and recoil back up the tree. Driven by instinct, the 2 **sloth vipers** (see **Appendix A: New Monsters**) never retreat and fight to the death to protect their offspring from falling into humanoid hands.

Tsathars

The insidious tsathars and cipatenhuas may share the same deity, but their animosity toward each other knows no bounds. The 1d4 + 3 **tsathars** (see **Appendix A: New Monsters**) believe themselves to be Tsathogga's children, relegating the cipatenhuas to unwelcome stepchildren. The crocodilian humanoids find the monstrous tsathars too deranged for their sensibilities. With this animosity in mind, this large team of tsathars has spent the last several weeks combing the area searching for the hidden shrine to their mad deity. In their warped minds, the cipatenhuas blaspheme their god, which requires them to find the concealed sanctum and corrupt it to their deranged way of thinking. Despite their exhaustive efforts, the entrance to the subterranean complex eludes them at every turn. If the characters encounter the tsathars during daylight hours, the monstrosities exhibit some caution moving about the area. They fan out across a wide perimeter, poking and prodding the ground with their spears in a feeble attempt to find the shrine through tactile examination. When the sun sets, the tsathars display their typical recklessness, blundering across the swamp in a frantic search for a cipatenhua who may lead them to their lair.

Regardless of the lighting conditions, the tsathars primarily rely on their keen sense of smell to detect nearby enemies. When they run across humanoids, the froglike creatures chaotically attack them with unbridled fury, throwing themselves at their foes like a wave crashing upon a beach. Without any leadership, the crazed tsathars attack the nearest creature until they kill it or the tsathar dies in the process of trying. If the characters capture a tsathar and can communicate with it, the prisoner reveals scant bits of information. The tsathar divulges that it hails from the Tlococua Marsh, south of the Great Canal bisecting the island, and that it was sent into the swamp to find the subterranean cipatenhua shrine. Otherwise, the demented tsathar rambles incoherently about demonic hordes of frogs ravaging the world.

Treasure: Each tsathar keeps a collection of humanoid finger bones and skeletal toes in a small bag that has no monetary value. One of the tsathars carries a silver earplug worth 50 gp.

Will-o'-wisps

Many adventurers have gone to their graves mistaking these dancing balls of malevolent light for natural phenomenon. To perpetrate this ruse, these undead abominations flicker and die out much like flammable swamp gas or bioluminescent insects trying to attract a mate. The monsters alternate between dimming their illumination and turning invisible while they approach living targets. When they shock their victims, the 1d3 **will-o'-wisps** quickly dart away in an effort to repeat the process. As the lingering essence of restless spirits, the undead creatures speak to the characters, lamenting their deaths in this forsaken place while reassuring the adventurers that they will keep them company when they join the will-o'-wisps in the next life. Despite their proclamations and arrogance, the malevolent beings retreat into the darkness if confronting a superior enemy. They watch and wait for another opportunity to attack the trespassers when they are preoccupied with another foe later in their journey.

Izmalli Swamp Set Encounters

This section describes three set encounters you can intersperse into the adventure to nudge the characters in the right direction during their search for the hidden shrine or to further challenge them along the way to their ultimate destination.

Pain and Gain

The cipatenhuas' newfound devotion to Tsathogga has not gone unnoticed. Six days ago, an **azizou (pain demon)** (see **Appendix A: New Monsters**) from the Abyss ventured to the island of Tehuatl to join the crocodilian humanoids in their quest to spread the demon prince's diabolical influence throughout the region. The hideous fiend accompanies a **cipatenhua disciple** (see **Appendix A: New Monsters**) on this malevolent journey through the wetlands. The demon uses its innate spellcasting to remain invisible throughout the trip while it visually scouts ahead for fresh souls to corrupt and torment. When the azizou locates a potential target, it non-verbally directs its companion to attack its prospective foes with its spells as it stealthily approaches a lone adversary to single out for an attack. When the characters first set eyes upon the demon, read or paraphrase the following description:

The cipatenhua disciple carries the heavy load in this combat as the scheming yet not physically powerful demon flits around in the treetops invisible as it waits for another opportunity to descend from the canopy and unleash its claws and teeth on an unsuspecting foe. Although the fiend desires to kill its quarry, it also seeks to corrupt them if it fails to do so. If combat turns against the pair, the demon coerces the cipatenhua disciple to surrender to the characters and lead them to the shrine where the azizou hopes to tempt them to evil later or murder them if they refuse while the odds are in the demon's favor. In this case, the azizou's cipatenhua guide leads the characters to the pond where the cipatenhuas enter the shrine, though it gives no further assistance or information about what awaits them in the tunnels and chambers ahead.

Treasure: The cipatenhua disciple has a hide bag containing two human skulls and a tsathar hip bone along with 3d6 gp that rattle around with these grisly trophies. The demon has a *potion of fire resistance* it took from a warlock.

ORG

For 17 years, Org the river troll has made his home along the banks of the Elcomatl River, living in a simple lean-to adjacent to a large tree. However, all is not as it appears. The distant town of Hrawrg planted an **oni** into the Izmalli Swamp to act as a spy for the Sepultudre, the septet of onis who rule that settlement. This oni known as Kerrogg merely plays the part of a river troll to the best of his ability. The solitary, misanthropic giant fervently hates the Aztlis and the other humanoids who inhabit the swamp, yet the outwardly feebleminded operative wisely avoids conflicts with the sentient creatures who cohabitate the region alongside him. He does not actively try to make friends out of the fear that appearing "too welcoming" may blow his cover, but he is also careful to avoid creating enemies as well. It takes considerable effort to crack through his acerbic outer shell, yet some local Aztli girls succeeded at the impossible by tapping into the seemingly oafish Kerrogg's perceived love for dance. Blessed with surprisingly nimble feet and an ear for rhythm, with the proper coaxing the giant sometimes joins the Aztli children for a routine they call "the river dance."

Kerrogg's joviality may feel spontaneous, but the covert agent has an ulterior motive for cultivating a "friendship" with the local Aztli children. The young girls enjoy chatting with the so-called "gentle" giant. They provide him a vital lifeline of information about the neighboring human settlements as well as details they overhear their parents discussing about the other people and creatures who inhabit the swamp. The observant giant also uses his eyes and ears to fill in the gaps, as he freely moves about the swamp with barely a second thought from most creatures, including the cipatenhuas who perceive him to be a harmless simpleton.

Naturally, the adventurers' unexpected appearance piques Kerrogg's interest, prompting him to actively yet discreetly seek them out. Kerrogg keeps his distance during his initial forays with the characters, yet when approached, he dons his typical ornery demeanor and keeps the newcomers at arm's length. Although he can certainly hold his own in a fight, Kerrogg would rather avoid bloodshed and work toward a shared goal of ridding the swamp of Tsathogga's blight. The oni has no love for the Aztlis and their gods, but if given a choice between siding with the humans he knows and the deranged cultists he loathes and secretly fears, the giant reluctantly takes sides with his human adversaries. However, it takes some effort to gain the oni's trust. Like the children, Kerrogg's guests can win his confidence with a successful DC 15 Charisma (Performance) check to imitate a version of his river dance.

Alternatively, the adventurers can attempt to logically reason with Kerrogg or bribe the oni into divulging information about the cipatenhuas' shrine and their activities. The giant is receptive to the characters' overtures for assistance. Therefore, it takes only a modest payment and/or a successful DC 15 Charisma (Persuasion) check to convince him to direct them to the shrine's hidden entrance. A suitable bribe with a value of 10 gp or more gives the character advantage on the preceding check, while a payment of 50 gp or more automatically garners his assistance. The characters can also attempt to ply him by sharing their information about other areas of the Izmalli Swamp, though if he senses the characters are fabricating information, he immediately terminates the conversation and demands they leave at once.

On the other hand, Kerrogg loathes taking orders from humans, especially if the adventurers try to bully him into giving them answers. In this case, an adventurer must succeed on a Charisma (Intimidation) check with disadvantage contested by Kerrogg's Wisdom (Insight) check. If the check fails, it takes a herculean effort for Kerrogg to give the characters a second chance. He demands they leave at once, and if they refuse, he gives them a frosty sendoff in the form of a *cone of cold* spell cast at them.

Of course, the characters may feel that peacefully interacting at all with an evil oni, regardless of his intentions in this matter, presents an unacceptable alternative, or they may simply see ridding Kerrogg from the swamp as an opportunity to kill two birds with one stone, i.e. eliminating a spy working for a sinister enterprise and looting his treasure. In this case, Kerrogg opts for flight over fight, and uses his abilities to turn invisible and transform into wispy vapors to escape the adventurers so he can plot his revenge at a later time. He may attempt to lure characters away from the group one at a time and kill them or change his appearance to infiltrate their ranks when they lower their defenses.

Treasure: Kerrogg sleeps in a simple lean-to along the riverbank but he keeps his worldly possessions on him at all times. He wears a ring of swimming on his left hand and has dust of dryness concealed in a gold locket worth 120 gp attached to a silver chain around his neck.

The Cat in the Hag's Hat

The dank recesses of the Izmalli Swamp offer refuge to some of Tehuatl's most malevolent denizens. Eltezcatl, a wicked **green hag**, clearly falls into the preceding category. Eltezcatl and her **hellcat** (see **Appendix A: New Monsters**) roam through the swamp from dusk until dawn, and there is a 50% chance of encountering them outdoors between mid-morning and late afternoon. If they are not here, the hag and her companion retreat to her abode, which is described later in this section. While venturing through the wilderness, the sly Eltezcatl dons the appearance of a young, vivacious, beautiful Aztli woman curiously walking across the wetlands with her pet cat who stays close to her side. During these daily jaunts, the seemingly carefree hag seeks young children to abduct and either adopt as her own or devour in one of her sickening stews. Her ideal quarry is a newborn or a pregnant woman, though neither of these individuals ever wanders through the swamp alone. Instead, the gregarious woman strikes up conversations with strangers in a subtle attempt to learn about any potential targets residing in the neighboring villages. She prefers speaking with teenagers and lone travelers rather than engaging groups of adults and especially armed warriors.

When Eltezcatl encounters adversaries who may pose a threat to her, she turns invisible and relies upon her cat companion to lure the characters toward the hag's home where a deadly trap awaits them. Indistinguishable from an ordinary housecat, the feline meows and cries as if it was vainly trying to tell the heroes something of great importance. It supplements these verbal cues by intentionally walking toward Eltezcatl's abode and keeping a sharp eye on the adventurers to make sure they are following. If the characters refuse to follow the clever aberration or ignore it altogether, the monster telepathically communicates to them that they are in great danger unless they obey the cat's instructions, though the cat makes it appear as if someone else is communicating that message.

The hag's thirst for mayhem is limitless, but her patience is not. Eltezcatl quickly wearies of the cat-and-mouse game, which causes her to drop all pretenses and viciously attack characters who refuse to play along with her and her hellcat. If this occurs, she lashes out with her savage claws while her feline companion uses its death gaze ability against what the monster perceives to be the greatest threat. When combat turns against the pair, they immediately dissolve their partnership and go their separate ways in a mad dash to escape the characters and save their miserable lives. In exchange for mercy, the hag and the hellcat are willing to barter information about the location of the cipatenhuas' shrine should the characters ask about it. While neither can pinpoint the exact spot or means of accessing the presumably subterranean compound, they can narrow it down to a much smaller one-square-mile area near the Elcomatl River. They also speculate that the entrance is submerged beneath a small body of water somewhere in that locale.

However, if the characters follow the hellcat to the hag's home, or alternatively, the characters stumble upon it on their own, they discover the sinister fey dwells in a cramped, universally shunned one-room cabin on the edge of a malodorous pond teeming with mosquitoes, leeches, gnats, and bestial scavengers that coalesce around its stinking waters. The roughly 400-square-foot structure has a barely functional door and is cluttered with junk Eltezcatl accumulated over the years. If the characters venture to her home, read or paraphrase the following description of her ramshackle abode's exterior:

> Vines, moss, and other vegetation wind their way up the brick walls of a dilapidated structure with a sloped, slate roof and a swollen wooden door fitted into the building's north side. Weeds, saplings, and shrubs grow unchecked on the grounds amid brooks and streams winding their way across the unkempt property.

A character who approaches the residence and succeeds on a DC 10 Wisdom (Perception) check notices the pungent scent of burnt tobacco lingering in the air. The door is not locked, but the excessive humidity makes the tight-fitting portal impossible to open without exerting some force. It takes a successful DC 10 Strength check to pull the door open. There are no other visible entrances. Read or paraphrase the following description to a character who peers into the structure's interior:

> Piles of filthy clayware and scraps of rotting food litter a disgusting table surrounded by four chairs. A straw pipe, tobacco scraps, and a ceramic bowl also sit atop the table. Mounds of refuse ranging from heaps of dirt and sand to warped branches to wooden containers of dried leaves cover almost the entirety of the floor, making it impossible to walk across the surface without stepping on an intervening object. A moldy, decomposing fur rests atop a crude bed stuffed against the far corner.

Eltezcatl's willingness to leave her presumably prized junk vulnerable to robbers feels out of character for the covetous hag, and that assumption is entirely correct. While most of these objects are worthless knickknacks she picked up over the years, the notion of someone else stealing a useless item from her rankles her to the core. Her primary guardian, a **wood golem** (see **Appendix A: New Monsters**), disguises itself as the table beneath a badly soiled cloth. If the construct hears a voice unaccompanied by Eltezcatl's shrill, the golem rises from its hiding spot, which signals an **animated jar** (see **Appendix A: New Monsters**) to also spring up from the floor and assault the intruders. The animated jar appears to be an ordinary jar even when subjected to thorough tactile examination. However, a successful DC 10 Wisdom (Perception) check determines the table's true nature if a character lifts up the tablecloth and looks underneath it. Otherwise, it takes a successful DC 20 Wisdom (Perception) check to notice the table wobbling slightly while being observed.

Treasure: Concealed amid the clutter within the home are a *spell scroll (witchbolt)*, *war paint (purple)* (see **Appendix B: New Items and Magic**), and two *potions of healing*. Eltezcatl keeps a *potion of greater healing* on her person along with a vial of *xochitl* (see **Appendix B: New Items and Magic**) and a gold ring inset with lapis lazuli stones worth 150 gp.

Finding the Shrine

The encounters in the preceding sections give the characters ample clues and assistance in locating the shrine or at least figuring out its probable location. Of course, the adventurers may also rely upon magic to aid them in their quest to root out the concealed shrine. Nonetheless, the heroes may still struggle to devise a feasible means of finding the entrance to Tsathogga's sanctum. If this is the case, you may have the characters encounter the cipatenhua sentries from the following section and give them an opportunity to question the guards about the shrine or use their tracking skills to follow them back to their lair. If the characters discover where to look for the shrine or determine its precise location, proceed to **Part Two** of the adventure.

Part Two: The Hidden Shrine of Tmocanotz

The clever cipatenhuas chose an ideal site to build their profane shrine. Situated roughly one-half mile north of the Elcomatl River, the proximity to the waterway grants them easy access to the river while also keeping them far enough from the riverbank to prevent other humanoids from bumbling into their lair accidentally. Nonetheless, the cipatenhuas maintain a vigilant watch over the surrounding area. If the characters venture within one mile of the cipatenhua stronghold, they have a 30% chance of encountering the sentries, including 3 **cipatenhuas** (see **Appendix A: New Monsters**) and a **crocodile**. If the cipatenhuas spot the characters first, they attempt to hide and ambush the adventurers when they move past them. Despite being indigenous to the area, the humanoids still treat the swamp as difficult terrain, though they partially overcome this deficiency with their ability to swim without impediment.

The preceding check is made at 10-minute intervals while the adventurers remain within a half-mile radius of the shrine. The characters cannot encounter more than two groups of sentries regardless of how long they remain in the area. Fearing death less than dishonor, the cipatenhuas never flee or surrender. If captured, they never willingly aid the characters, though they can be magically compelled to divulge logistical details about their lair or they can be forced to do so with successful Charisma checks as discussed in the **Abduction** adventure hook.

Treasure: The cipatenhuas carry a total of 2d6 blue quartz stones (worth 10 gp each) in addition to their listed weapons and armor. One of them also has a pouch containing 4d6 sp and 3d6 gp in addition to a small bronze idol (worth 25 gp) of a gar-like fish. The object has no religious or cultural significance to the cipatenhua, who simply acquired it from an earlier kill.

If the characters successfully circumvent the stronghold's outer sentries, the guards stationed outside the entrance to the cipatenhua stronghold await them.

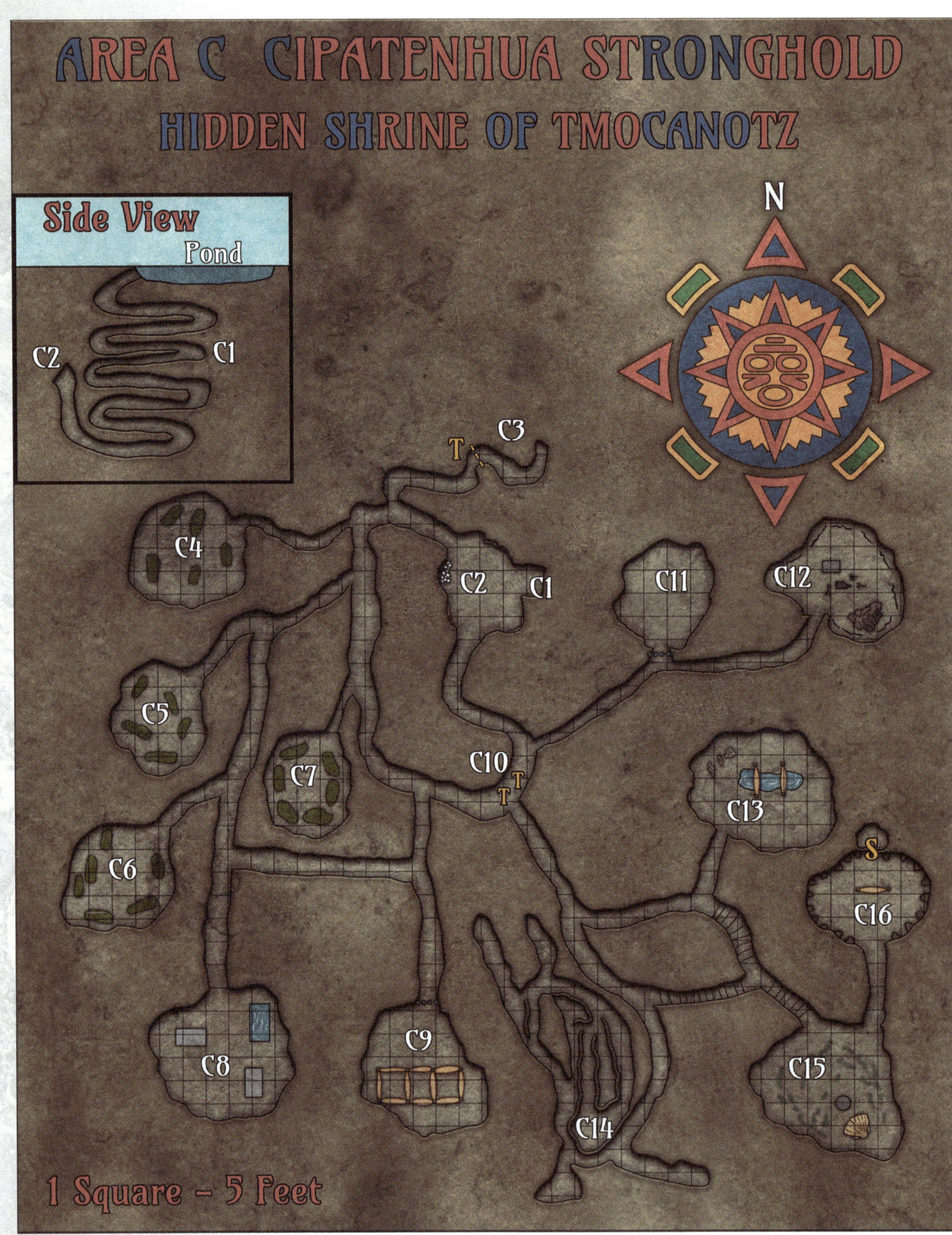

AREA C CIPATENHUA STRONGHOLD
HIDDEN SHRINE OF TMOCANOTZ
N
Side View
Pond
C2
C1
C3
T
C4
C2
C1
C11
C12
C5
C7
C10
T
T
C13
C6
S
C16
C8
C9
C15
C14
1 Square - 5 Feet

These 4 **cipatenhuas** (see **Appendix A: New Monsters**) savagely attack any trespassers who venture close to their lair. If the characters approach this area, read or paraphrase the following description:

Unlike the sentries, the guards emit ear-piercing shrieks to alert the cipatenhuas in the submerged entrance of their subterranean stronghold along the edge of a mossy fen. Furthermore, they never retreat into their lair, forcing the characters to devise a method of locating the submerged entrance at the western edge of the pond behind them.

Treasure: The cipatenhuas each carry a pouch containing 1d3 obsidian stones (worth 10 gp each) in addition to their listed gear and equipment.

The pond's murky waters conceal the submerged entrance to the cipatenhuas' stronghold, but the surrounding area reveals several important clues. A successful DC 10 Wisdom (Survival) check reveals numerous footprints around the water's edge. More importantly, a check that succeeds by 5 or more also indicates that the tracks lead into and out of the pond rather than move around its edges. The earth around the pond's edges is soft and spongy, but the ground farther away from the pond is yielding but not soggy. A character can discover this curious detail through tactile examination or by succeeding on a DC 15 Intelligence (Investigation) check. Armed with this knowledge, the character realizes the area is slightly elevated, meaning the pond is not fed by groundwater seeping up to the surface. Likewise, a character who succeeds on a DC 10 Intelligence (Nature) check recognizes the pond as a fen fed exclusively by precipitation and runoff from other locations rather than groundwater. A character who puts these pieces together may deduce that the pond opens into a subterranean complex. Alternatively, a character who succeeds on a DC 15 Intelligence check reaches the same conclusion, regardless of how they discovered the possibility of an underground chamber.

If the characters reach the preceding epiphany, they are faced with the dilemma of finding the entrance to the tunnel. The small pond encompasses an area measuring only 200 square feet and is a mere four feet deep at its nadir. Although drowning in the shallow water is an unlikely possibility, the murky water obscures all sight, effectively rendering characters blind while underwater. A character who takes the plunge into the water can use their hands to probe around the bottom of the pond, while a character who succeeds on a DC 15 Wisdom (Perception) check notices the water current flows from east to west, indicating the presence of a subterranean tunnel.

Cipatenhua Shrine Features

Naturally, the cipatenhuas designed their stronghold to accommodate them rather than unwelcome visitors. The humanoids packed damp moss onto the walls and ceilings to limit the amount of water entering the complex. However, unless otherwise stated in an area's description, enough liquid seeps through the imperfect system to soak the earthen floor in roughly 1d2 + 1 feet of standing water, making the entire stronghold difficult terrain, though a creature with a swim speed can move through the corridors and passages uninhibited. The ceilings are 1d4 + 4 feet in height in each separate chamber and passageway. Creatures too tall to stand upright must spend an additional foot of movement to move one foot and suffer disadvantage on attack rolls and Dexterity saving throws made in the area. Opponents have advantage on attack rolls made against creatures too large to move about without crouching or stooping. Furthermore, darkness envelops the entire stronghold unless otherwise mentioned in an area's description.

C1: Submerged Tunnel

The decaying organic matter covering the walls impedes the flow of groundwater into the completely submerged, four-foot-diameter underground pipe that descends at a consistent 30-degree angle until it reaches a depth of 25 feet before the tunnel makes a sharp 10-foot-long U-bend. In total, the tunnel traverses a distance of 105 feet, which presents two problems. While the nimble cipatenhuas can easily hold their breath in an aquatic environment and swim through the tight space, larger humanoids weighed down by armor and bulky equipment fare much worse. Furthermore, the cipatenhuas know the passage's twists and turns by heart; the characters almost certainly have no knowledge of the tunnel's length nor its dimensions.

Unless a character has a swim speed, the passage makes for tight quarters for a Medium-sized creature to conventionally swim through it, though Small-sized and tinier creatures who succeed on a DC 10 Strength (Athletics) check can swim through the tunnel at half their normal speed as usual. Medium-sized creatures can attempt to swim through the area, but do so with disadvantage. Any creature larger than Medium-sized is too big to squeeze into the narrow space at all. A creature that foregoes or fails a Strength (Athletics) check made to swim through the tunnel may instead crawl through it with the passageway being treated as difficult terrain. It costs a character three feet of movement to move one foot under these difficult circumstances.

The murky water completely blinds adventurers and prevents them from breathing. A character can hold its breath for a number of minutes equal to 1 + its Constitution modifier (minimum of 30 seconds). Compounding the problem is the fact that the character is attempting to negotiate a path through a winding, narrow tunnel in cloudy water that obscures all types of vision. While characters might normally be able to use their hands to grope around in the darkness to find their way, in this instance, characters must use their hands to help them crawl along the ground. At each of the eight bends in the tunnel, you may require a character to succeed on a DC 10 Wisdom (Perception) check to sense the upcoming turn. On a failed check, the character must use an action to figure out the tunnel's new direction. On a success, the character continues crawling or swimming without stopping.

When the character reaches the U-bend at the end of the tunnel, handholds and footholds along the tunnel walls aid creatures climbing up the vertical shaft opening into area **C2**. It takes a successful DC 5 Strength (Athletics) check to scale the surface. Alternatively, creatures with a swim speed can reach the top of the U-bend without succeeding on a skill check. When a character reaches the top of the U-bend, a successful DC 5 Strength (Athletics) check is again needed to hoist the creature out of the water and onto the platform in the adjoining chamber.

C2: Cipatenhua Guard Chamber

No respite awaits characters who complete the grueling slog through the watery tunnel, though there are only small pools of standing water covering the floor rather than being mired in difficult terrain. Waiting to unceremoniously greet them are 6 **cipatenhuas** (see **Appendix A: New Monsters**) who stand at the ready to surprise any intruders who emerge from the tunnel. The clever creatures make a loud commotion that alerts attentive listeners within the complex. However, no reinforcements ever arrive to assist the cipatenhuas at this location. The cipatenhuas never retreat and fight until killed.

The cipatenhuas piled 39 humanoid skulls onto the heap of decapitated heads against the far wall. A character who examines the remains and succeeds on a DC 10 Wisdom (Medicine) check confirms that a sharp instrument severed the heads from the attached vertebrae. Likewise, a successful DC 10 Intelligence (Nature) check confirms the racial identity of each victim. In all, there are 29 humans, three orcs, two gnolls, two elves, two dwarves, and one halfling. In each case, it takes one round to thoroughly examine the earthly remains.

The three abstract images painted on the organic medium attached to the walls vaguely depict a grotesque amphibian beast with slimy skin, webbed appendages, and a frog's head. However, the artwork appears crude and of poor quality, making it difficult to decipher its subject. Nonetheless, a character who succeeds on a DC 15 Intelligence (Religion) check can pick out enough details in the painting to determine that it appears to be a depiction of Tsathogga, though it differs from tsathar portraits of their insane deity. In another disturbing development, a successful DC 10 Intelligence (Nature) check confirms that the medium the artworks are painted on is indeed human rather than animal flesh.

Treasure: Each cipatenhua has a pouch containing 1d4 blue quartz stones (worth 10 gp each) in addition to their listed armor and weaponry.

C3: Trapped Passageway

The cipatenhuas never venture down this trapped corridor as they intended it to ensnare trespassers exploring their territory. To further entice intruders into venturing down the hallway, the area is normal terrain, making it easy for characters to walk down the slightly elevated passageway. When the characters reach the dotted line marked as "T", read or paraphrase the following description:

The cipatenhuas deliberately packed excrement and other methane producing materials at the far end of the bend to build up concentrations of the gas in that bend. To prevent the methane gas from spreading beyond this corridor, the cipatenhuas installed hidden vents in the ceiling that allow the gas to flow out of the complex to the surface. It takes a successful DC 20 Wisdom (Perception) check to spot the eight tiny holes bored into the ceiling and walls from the beginning of the corridor to the "T" location.

Methane Trap

At room temperature, combustible methane gas is colorless and odorless, though the manure emits a foul stench. A pressure plate in the floor at the dotted line marked as "T" creates a spark that ignites the explosive methane.

If the trap is triggered, all creatures within 20 feet of the pressure plate must make a DC 10 Dexterity saving throw. On a failure, a creature takes 21 (6d6) fire damage while on a success a creature takes half as much damage. If an explosion occurs, the cipatenhuas residing in area **C4** race to the scene to investigate.

A successful DC 15 Wisdom (Perception) check or Intelligence (Investigation) check locates the pressure plate. A successful DC 15 Dexterity check made with thieves' tools disarms the pressure plate. However, a spark or flame from a different source such as a lit torch or *fire bolt* still detonates the methane gas trap even if the characters disarmed the triggering mechanism. In this case, the blast is centered on the ignition source rather than the pressure plate.

C4: Cipatenhua Living Quarters

Only 2 **cipatenhuas** (see **Appendix A: New Monsters**) currently occupy these living quarters while their colleagues tend to sentry and guard duties. If they hear an explosion in area **C3**, they rush out to investigate the matter. Otherwise, the pair happily feasts on meat plucked from the exoskeletal chunks taken from a giant crab. They remain engrossed in eating until they notice the characters or until the characters interrupt their meal. They then leap to their feet to attack. It takes a successful DC 15 Intelligence (Nature) check to identify the chitinous pieces as the severed legs of a giant crab. Likewise, a successful DC 10 Intelligence (Nature) check identifies the vegetation doubling for beds as seaweed.

Treasure: The cipatenhuas hide their belongings underneath the seaweed. A character who pokes around in each individual seaweed bed finds 1d4 bloodstones (10 gp each) with a successful DC 5 Wisdom (Perception) check.

C5: Cipatenhua Living Quarters

The four cipatenhuas and cipatenhua disciple who reside here are currently on guard and sentry duties, leaving their quarters unoccupied. Being suspicious of their fellow cipatenhuas, these humanoids left nothing behind for the others to steal. A successful DC 10 Intelligence (Nature) check identifies the vegetation doubling for beds as seaweed.

C6: Cipatenhua Living Quarters

This chamber is surprisingly dry compared to most others, with only a thin coating of water covering the floor and is not treated as difficult terrain. The 2 **cipatenhuas** (see **Appendix A: New Monsters**) and **cipatenhua disciple** (see **Appendix A: New Monsters**) who dwell here bide their time toying with 2 **poisonous snakes** they recently captured. Before devouring them, the trio cruelly taunts the animals. With their attention focused solely on their prey, creatures attempting to go unnoticed gain advantage on Dexterity (Stealth) checks made to avoid being detected by the distracted cipatenhuas. However, if the cipatenhuas spot the characters, they refocus their attention on the trespassers in their midst. Otherwise, they continue to torment the snakes until the characters rudely break up their extended play session. It takes a successful DC 10 Intelligence (Nature) check to identify the vegetation doubling for beds as seaweed.

Treasure: The cipatenhuas hide their belongings underneath the seaweed. A character who pokes around in each individual seaweed bed finds 2d6 gp scattered inside it with a successful DC 5 Wisdom (Perception) check.

C7: Cipatenhua Living Quarters

The two cipatenhuas and three cipatenhua disciples who normally dwell in these quarters are currently outside the stronghold on a hunting excursion. The occupants took their treasures with them, though one of the cipatenhuas hid a curious item within her bedroll. The object is described in the **Treasure** section. A successful DC 10 Intelligence (Nature) check identifies the vegetation doubling for beds as seaweed.

In their absence, a **demonic mist** (see **Appendix A: New Monsters**) loiters in the otherwise empty living quarters. During the cipatenhuas' last sacrificial rite, the frog priests overseeing the ceremony tapped into the netherworld's entropic energy, which summoned this abyssal monstrosity to this world. The creature blended its misty form into the seaweed, giving it advantage on its Stealth check. When the characters enter the room, the demonic mist waits for them to let down their guard before it rises from the muck and blasts the adventurers with a *fear* spell. It then wades into combat using its Demonic Touch and Psychic Crush attacks to slaughter its foes. If significantly damaged, reduced to one-half its maximum hit points or fewer, the demonic mist resorts to casting *vampiric touch* to regain some of its lost hit points. In a bind, the monster passes through the walls and retreats deeper into the complex, moving toward area **C15** where it alerts the frog prince to the presence of intruders and waits for the characters inside the clam shell in the cipatenhua shrine.

Treasure: The seaweed bed in the southwestern portion of the room contains a small bronze sculpture of a jaguar (worth 50 gp). The cipatenhua understood the object's religious significance, which prompted her to carefully hide the potentially blasphemous item from her fellow cipatenhuas. Therefore, it takes a successful DC 15 Wisdom (Perception) check to locate the bronze artwork. It takes a successful DC 5 Intelligence (Religion) check to associate the cat with the Aztli god Itztliteotl.

C8: Mess Hall

Light from torches ensconced in the walls illuminates the chamber. Dim light extends roughly 15 feet into the tunnel outside the chamber. The floor is wet but not covered in water.

The unpleasant task of butchering the giant crab on the stone slab falls to the three slaves (LN male and female human [Aztli] **commoners** armed with itzopillis [see **Appendix B: New Items and Magic**] instead of clubs) who toil under the brutal direction of 3 **cipatenhuas** (see **Appendix A: New Monsters**) and a **cipatenhua disciple** (see **Appendix A: New Monsters**). Although armed with butchering implements, the three abused slaves lack the combat training and physical stamina to fight back against their captors. The cipatenhuas ignore the slaves, redirecting their attention to the intruders. The cipatenhua disciple attempts to tip over the stone basin near the entrance, a feat requiring him to succeed on a DC 15 Strength check. If he accomplishes this task, he releases a **swarm of poisonous snakes** that indiscriminately attacks the nearest creature. Obviously, the cipatenhua disciple makes sure to tip the basin away from him and closer to his enemies, though doing so proves to be an inexact science. After one failed attempt, the cipatenhua disciple abandons the effort and attacks the characters with his repertoire of warlock spells until he exhausts them.

The male slaves, Itzatl and Nectli, along with their female counterpart Zyotia, were captured while traveling along a well-worn path with 11 others roughly four months ago. Throughout their captivity, they have been systemically tortured, beaten, and malnourished. Six of the group's traveling companions perished from starvation or mistreatment, while the cipatenhuas presumably sacrificed the other five to their malevolent deity, whom they refer to as the "Ciuatl," which translates as frog. The slaves cannot accurately gauge their captors' numerical strength or provide details about the complex other than the mess hall and their filthy quarters in area **C9**. However, they know their overseers ultimately answer to a priest or some other religious figure who leads the savage humanoids and may hold additional slaves. In addition, the cipatenhuas keep at least one or two giant crabs in a holding tank somewhere in the subterranean complex.

C9: Slaves' Quarters

A rudimentary latticework carved from wood and reinforced with bronze prevents unfettered entrance into the slaves' quarters. The cipatenhuas bolted the device into the doorjamb from the outside. The apparatus can be disengaged from the door frame with a successful DC 15 Dexterity check made with thieves' tools or it can be forced open with a successful DC 20 Strength check. Dim light from torches ensconced into the wall extends 15 feet into the outer hallway, bathing the slaves' quarters in normal light. The corridor outside the chamber ascends slightly before opening into this area. The earthen floor in the chamber is wet but not covered with water; thus, the chamber is not treated as difficult terrain.

These spartan quarters provide sleeping accommodations for 10 individuals, though the three slaves currently occupying area **C8** are the only individuals living here. However, a character who succeeds on a DC 5 Intelligence (Investigation) check surmises the quantity of items and bodily waste littering the ground confirms that more than three people once dwelt in these crowded quarters. Otherwise, a thorough search of the slaves' quarters reveals nothing of significance.

C10: Trapped Corridor

This juncture connects the living quarters on the western side of the complex with the religious center and work areas in the eastern section. The water here varies between three and four feet in depth, making it easy for cipatenhuas to swim across the water's surface through the intersection containing pit traps triggered by the creature's weight.

Concealed Pit Trap

The cipatenhuas scattered three pit traps throughout this stretch of the corridor. The five-foot-diameter, 30-foot-deep cylindrical pit traps are neatly concealed beneath dirt and other debris scattered on the floor underneath the water. The hinges supporting the traps give way only when subjected to 125 pounds of direct pressure on the spot, which allows the cipatenhuas to harmlessly swim over them without triggering the traps. Likewise, when they parade a giant crab to the mess hall for butchering, the large crustacean is too big to fall into the round hole bored into the ground. In essence, the cipatenhuas' traps are tailormade to capture humans and other Medium humanoids trespassing into their territory.

If the trap is triggered, the creature who steps on the hinged door must succeed on a DC 10 Dexterity saving throw or fall into the pit, taking 10 (3d6) bludgeoning damage from the plunge and an additional 7 (2d6) slashing damage from shards of obsidian imbedded in the floor. The spring supporting the hinged, watertight door then slams back into place. To make matters worse, the shaft fills with 1d4 feet of water. It takes a successful DC 10 Strength check to reopen the door from inside or outside the pit. Alternatively, placing 125 pounds of direct pressure on the door is sufficient to reopen it as well, though the door springs shut again if the weight is removed and quickly fills with water, which could potentially drown a creature at the bottom of the shaft. A creature stuck at the bottom of the pit can climb out with a successful DC 10 Strength (Athletics) check.

A successful DC 20 Wisdom (Perception) check or Intelligence (Investigation) check locates the traps concealed in the floor, and the latter check also determines the conditions necessary to trigger the traps. A successful DC 15 Dexterity check made with thieves' tools disarms a concealed pit trap.

C11: Food Supply

Four sets of brackets affixed to the outer walls of the entrance support long wooden poles that function as makeshift cell bars. The poles comfortably sit inside the brackets, forming a secure pen for the creature trapped inside while allowing someone who can manipulate objects to easily remove the poles without succeeding on any checks.

> A rudimentary cell door constructed from bronze brackets and wooden poles prevents unfettered egress from a holding pen.

During their periodic raids, the cipatenhuas capture giant crabs and venomous snakes for later consumption. The humanoids currently keep a **giant crab** captive in this holding tank, which is partially filled with water. The beast attacks any creature foolish enough to enter its domain. If the characters are intent on killing the overgrown crustacean without risking injury to themselves, they can fire ranged weapons between the wooden poles that act as bars. However, in this circumstance, you can opt to award the characters fewer experience points for essentially shooting a fish in a barrel.

C12: Armory

A character who succeeds on a DC 10 Wisdom (Perception) check immediately after passing area **C11** hears the distinct sound of metal striking metal and sees dim light originating from the armory. The floor in this area is wet but not submerged beneath water as it is slightly elevated and has drains running along the edge of the floor. If the character spends at least one minute in the hallway observing and listening, a successful DC 15 Wisdom (Perception) check also overhears voices. A character who speaks Dwarvish recognizes the language's inflections as Dwarvish but cannot discern what is being said amid the cacophony of clanging hammers.

> Two sooty male dwarves pound away at a piece of molten metal atop an anvil, while a third member of the team monitors a nearby kiln. Water, presumably from the swamp or pond above the complex, cascades down the walls from cracks in the ceiling and then drains into even wider fissures in the floor along the room's edges. Two bronze battleaxes rest on the floor near the kiln along with metal forceps. Rags heaped along the near wall presumably function as crude bedding for the occupants.

The three dwarven metalworkers (N male dwarf **commoners** armed with light hammers instead of clubs) tirelessly work under the direction of 2 **cipatenhua disciples** (see **Appendix A: New Monsters**) and a **cipatenhua frog priest** (see **Appendix A: New Monsters**) who intently watch while the dwarven team of Dhumgurin, Erinri, and Vormic Harlbrun feverishly forge his ceremonial bronze dagger. If the characters intrude on the dwarves' efforts, the frog priest emits its Crazed Croak attack to prevent spellcasters from using spells requiring concentration and to make the character more vulnerable to some of his spells. If successful, the frog priest then casts *bestow curse* and *hold person* against susceptible opponents. If unsuccessful, the frog priest instead casts *shield of faith* to bolster his defenses and *spiritual weapon* to attack his foes from distance. If the characters surround him or bear down on

him too quickly to safely use his spells, he attacks with his bite and greatclub. The deranged frog priest continually babbles throughout the battle and hurls bizarre insults at any Aztli adversaries, especially those who venerate Itztliteotl. He verbally expresses his desire to "feast on their putrid entrails," "clamp his jaws down onto their luscious flesh," and "spill their blood for the Ciuatl's lecherous tongue." He emits an unnerving croaking laugh between these illogical phrases while waiting for his crazed croak to recharge.

Meanwhile, the two cipatenhua disciples unleash their most potent magic at their enemies, blasting characters with their ranged spells before engaging them in melee combat. The disciples demand the heroes surrender to Tsathogga and comment that the demon prince would enjoy watching their crispy flesh roasting over an open fire. The dwarves stand their ground yet make no deliberate attempts to join in the combat. However, if one of them is adjacent to the same foe as a character, the emboldened dwarf takes a swing at his captor. Vormic, the dwarf currently holding the hot molten rod in his forceps, tries to hit one of the cipatenhuas with the searing object, which functions as an improvised weapon dealing 1d6 fire damage in addition to its normal damage.

The cipatenhuas captured the three dwarven cousins approximately three months ago. Although they live in squalor, the malevolent humanoids treat these skilled artisans far better than their menial human laborers. Despite receiving full rations of food, less direct oversight, and avoiding regular abuse at the cipatenhuas' hands, the dwarves long to escape their captivity. However, they have never ventured past area **C10** and have had contact only with the frog priest and his cipatenhua underlings. However, they believe the frog priest answers to a higher authority within the complex.

The kiln reaches a maximum temperature high enough to forge bronze, but insufficient to smelt iron. The oven contains most of the heat internally, while the chilly water cascading down the walls operates as a natural air conditioning unit.

C13: Frog Priest Quarters

Unlike the other areas in this complex, the ceiling in this chamber reaches a height of 12 feet, with the hammocks suspended six feet above the ground.

> Four wooden poles embedded into the ground support two hammocks stretched across a pool of murky water covering a large portion of the floor. Two conch horns and a closed scallop shell rest on the floor against the near corner.

While one of the complex's two frog priests oversees the dwarves' activities in area **C12**, the other **cipatenhua frog priest** (see **Appendix A: New Monsters**) peacefully sleeps in the hammock suspended over the pool. The seemingly helpless cipatenhua frog priest appears to be at the characters' mercy as he blissfully dreams of wanton slaughter. Indeed, the adventurers have advantage on Dexterity (Stealth) checks made to approach him without him noticing the advancing opponents. However, the frog priest is not alone. A **swarm of poisonous frogs** (see **Appendix A: New Monsters**) occupies the pool beneath the hammocks, which are intentionally placed three feet above the water. The poisonous frogs do not attack the cipatenhua frog priest. The hungry beasts hide in the cloudy waters of the four-foot-deep pond, granting the collective advantage on its Dexterity (Stealth) check to remain unnoticed. The cipatenhua frog priests trained the frogs to remain within the pond to act as a potential food source and as guardians. Nonetheless, when creatures other than the cipatenhuas come within five feet of the pool's edges, the swarm emerges from the muck to feed if it detects their presence, most likely through its sense of smell if the area remains dark. The mindless frogs cannot discern the cipatenhua frog priest from other creatures, though the swarm generally attacks the first creature it detects, other than the cipatenhuas, and continues to envelop that foe until it slays the hapless victim and moves onto the next closest target. Fully aware of the swarm's tendencies, the frog priest keeps his distance from the frogs whenever possible.

Treasure: The frog priests keep their baubles and curiosities inside the conch horns and oversized scallop shell. One conch horn contains six silver nuggets (worth 10 gp each) and four tin nuggets (worth 1 gp). The second conch horn holds 35 gp and two garnets (worth 100 gp each). It takes a successful DC 5 Strength check to pry open the scallop shell. The characters find seven pearls (worth 100 gp each), an *arrow of flesh finding* (see **Appendix B: New Items and Magic**) and a *potion of growth*.

C14: Mine

Crudely cut passages carved into the earth and stone create a honeycomb of soggy yet not deluged corridors and chambers in a confined area. Loose chunks of rock and soil litter the floor alongside the occasional chisel or pick.

The dwarves toiling in area **C12** occasionally venture into these twisting, wet mine shafts to extract raw materials from the exposed rock to forge objects in the cipatenhuas' foundry. A character who succeeds on a DC 10 Intelligence check identifies the metals protruding from the cut surfaces as tin, brass, and iron with small deposits of agate stones. A character who spends an hour chipping away searching for these materials recovers 4d6 gp worth of metal and gems up to a maximum of 40d6 gp of materials yielded for all characters, though the noise may attract the attention of cipatenhuas and creatures in other areas. The dwarves and cipatenhuas who oversee them keep their distance from the 4 **t'shanns** (see **Appendix A: New Monsters**) who burrow through the walls and floors blissfully devouring any minerals embedded within the dirt and rocks. The small, slug-like creatures secrete powerful digestive enzymes that dissolve stone and allow them to burrow through these materials. The t'shanns are not aggressive. They monitor the activities of trespassers from afar if they detect them, though they take no actions to directly avoid them or attack them. However, merely approaching within 30 feet of these strange creatures may remove any self-control the characters may have. The strange thoughts sifting through the t'shanns' brains inadvertently affect the actions of sentient creatures. If the characters intentionally or unintentionally attack the t'shanns, the aberrations fight back to the death.

C15: Cipatenhua Shrine

The sounds of bizarre chanting and the rancid stench of decay fill the area outside the intersections branching off to areas **C13** and **C14**. A character who succeeds on a DC 10 Wisdom (Perception) check can hear and smell the preceding effects. Characters roll the preceding check separately only if they have advantage or disadvantage for one, but not both, of these senses. In addition, the passages outside the shrine descend at a decline between 15 and 30 degrees, a characteristic all characters notice.

Strands of greenish-black seaweed dangle from the ceiling. The stringy vegetation wraps around long, thin pieces of bone. Blood, tissue, and bodily fluids stain a round stone pedestal with a serrated, stone blade resting atop the gruesome surface. Behind the pedestal, a collection of larger bones and clearly humanoid skulls reside inside a large, half-open clam shell that has been retrofitted into the likeness of a frog's gaping maw. A portion of a fleshy tongue dangles over the shell's lip.

The brutal cipatenhuas disembowel their victims on the round pedestal and hurl their organs and entrails into the open clam shell where they slowly rot and decay amid their scraped larger bones. The wicked creatures then attach their finger bones to the strands of seaweed hanging from the ceiling. Although the pieces of vegetation affixed to the ceiling are not bunched close enough together to form a contiguous curtain, the strips of solid material are present in sufficient numbers to cause the shrine to be a lightly obscured area imposing disadvantage on Wisdom (Perception) checks that rely on sight.

The 2 **cipatenhua disciples** (see **Appendix A: New Monsters**) and Griigg, the **cipatenhua frog prince** (see **Appendix A: New Monsters**) who rules the complex, engage in rhythmic chanting, though they have no victim to sacrifice at the moment. A character who succeeds on a DC 15 Wisdom (Insight) check determines that the trio are currently participating in a war chant rather than a religious ritual, while a character who succeeds on a DC 15 Intelligence (Religion) check associates the cipatenhuas' cadence with the chants performed by Tsathogga's followers. The cipatenhua frog prince was in the act of inspiring the cipatenhua disciples to venture back onto the surface to retrieve more victims for their vicious rites when the characters presumably crash their party. Despite their intense focus, the cipatenhuas' passive Perception remains unaffected. If the **demonic mist** (see **Appendix A: New Monsters**) from area **C7** retreated here, the cipatenhuas have advantage on Wisdom (Perception) checks. The incorporeal monster hides within the frog's gaping maw. The creature emerges after 1d2 rounds of combat and joins the fray alongside Tsathogga's deranged minions. However, if the characters defeat the frog prince, the monster flees again, racing back toward the surface in an effort to flee the shrine altogether and wreak mayhem elsewhere in the swamp.

When the cipatenhuas finally notice the intrusion, the triad springs into action and unleashes a flooded room trap designed to even the odds against their land-based foes. As the water fills the chamber, they leap into the water and attack the characters with their melee weapons. The frog prince loudly boasts of Tsathogga's greatness and curses Itztliteotl as the blasphemous god who condemned his people to the island's dank marshes and swamps. He decries his longing to walk among the grasses and climb the highest peaks yet spends his days in a bleak, subterranean world. Griigg boasts that his offerings of flesh and blood have earned him the Frog God's favor when his demonic servants walk the earth and spread pain and suffering across the land. Despite his physical strength, Griigg has less magical power than his counterparts. He rushes into battle wildly swinging his greatclub at an injured character against whom he is most effective.

The disciples fight as a team, targeting the enemy they deem to be the physically weakest or who is obviously the smallest opponent. They begin the onslaught with their spells and then move in for the kill against their designated adversary. The cipatenhua disciples never surrender or retreat with their leader present, though they may attempt to flee if the characters kill the frog prince first. Otherwise, the trio fights to the death.

FLOODED CHAMBER TRAP

The cipatenhuas deliberately placed their shrine at a lower depth than the remainder of their complex to allow them to rapidly fill the room with water. To activate the trap, one of the cipatenhuas must sharply tug on a strand of tightly wrapped copper cable just above the rounded stone painted to resemble a strand of seaweed. It takes a successful DC 10 Strength check to pull down the cable and open a watertight trapdoor built into the ceiling. When the portal opens, water rapidly pours into the room at a rate of 1d3 feet per round up to a maximum depth of four feet. Creatures submerged beneath the water may eventually drown or suffer disadvantage on their attack rolls. Furthermore, creatures who lack a swimming speed treat the water as difficult terrain.

The water deals no damage, but on the round when the water first rushes into the room, all characters in the shrine must succeed on a DC 10 Strength check at the beginning of their turn or be knocked prone. A successful DC 15 Wisdom (Perception) check allows the character to detect the trapdoor built into the ceiling and the attached concealed copper cable amid the seaweed.

The cipatenhuas use the round stone, which the characters can identify as quartz with a successful DC 5 Intelligence check, to perform their grisly rites. Much like the indigenous Aztlis who perform ritualistic humanoid sacrifices, the cipatenhuas use the flint dagger on the stone to remove their victims' internal organs in an offering to Tsathogga. The desecrated altar radiates a faint aura of necromancy magic. A living creature who touches or comes into physical contact with the stone must succeed on a DC 8 Wisdom saving throw or take 3 (1d6) necrotic damage and be stunned until the end of its next turn while experiencing a vision depicting countless hordes of frogs inhabiting a bleak, subterranean cavern stretching for miles in every direction. The round stone is an object that can be damaged or destroyed. It has AC 15 and 50 hit points. Reducing the stone to 0 hit points destroys it and dispels the magical aura enchanting it.

The clam shell adjacent to the stone contains an assortment of skulls, vertebrae, and long bones harvested from dozens of individuals as well as a faux tongue stitched together from excess sinew and muscle repurposed from their victims' bodies. The mollusk carapace measures almost eight feet in length and is four feet wide and four feet high. An adventurer who sifts through the assortment of skeletal remains and succeeds on a DC 10 Intelligence (Nature) check confirms that the overwhelming majority of the remains are of human origin.

C16: FROG PRINCE'S QUARTERS

In an unusual twist, the cipatenhua frog prince collected his adversaries' pelvic bones as macabre trophies. Most are intact, though some are broken in half or fragmented into smaller pieces. It is impossible to associate the skeletal remains with any specific individuals, though an examination of the 43 pelvises and a successful DC 10 Intelligence (Nature) check determines that almost all of them are human and roughly half of them are female. The hammock is spun from silk, making it very unusual and rare.

The frog prince conceals his treasure behind one of the niches. It takes a successful DC 15 Wisdom (Perception) check to spot the outline of a panel, though the character must then succeed on a DC 15 Intelligence (Investigation) check to ascertain that twisting the eastern pole supporting the hammock one full rotation counterclockwise opens the niche.

Treasure: The characters can disentangle the frog prince's silk hammock (worth 50 gp) from its supports with a successful DC 5 Dexterity check made with tools. The small niche behind the secret panel holds a leather pouch containing 423 gp and six corals (worth 100 gp each). There is also a *folding boat* disguised as a wooden box, a *potion of giant strength* (hill), a *cuacalalatli of the beast (frog)* (see **Appendix B: New Items and Magic**) taken from a trespasser, and a *ring of water walking*, also removed from the finger of a former adventurer.

CONCLUDING THE ADVENTURE

If you used this adventure as a side trek for ***The Re-education of Coyotl***, the characters have rid the Izmalli Swamp of the Tsathogga-worshipping branch of the cipatenhuas who recently migrated to the wetland and may proceed back to Teohuacan to investigate the events at the calmecac. If the characters defeated Griigg and his two frog priests, any remaining cipatenhuas in the region ultimately disperse back to their marsh without their religious leaders. However, unless the characters destroy the altar in area **C15**, the tsathars locate the hidden shrine in 1d3 weeks and repopulate the unholy site venerating Tsathogga. In a strange twist, Org, the oni masquerading as a river troll, seeks out the adventurers who destroyed Tsathogga's enclave and offers them safe passage to his home settlement in the Tepepan Mountains if the need to visit ever arises. The characters are also free to use this adventure as the launching point for the preceding adventure as one of the freed slaves may ask the characters to escort him or her back home to the neighboring town.

Appendix A: New Monsters

The following monsters are found in this adventure:

Animated Jar
Tiny construct, unaligned

Armor Class 14**Hit Points** 28 (8d4 + 8)
Speed 20 ft., fly 30 ft. (hover)

STR	DEX	CON	INT	WIS	CHA
10 (+0)	18 (+4)	13 (+1)	1 (–5)	5 (–3)	1 (–5)

Saving Throws Dexterity +6
Skills Perception –1
Damage Immunities poison, psychic
Condition Immunities blinded, charmed, deafened, exhaustion, frightened, paralyzed, petrified, poisoned
Senses blindsight 60 ft. (blind beyond this radius), passive Perception 9
Languages —
Challenge 1/2 (100 XP)

Antimagic Susceptibility. The animated object is incapacitated while in the area of an *antimagic field*. If targeted by *dispel magic*, the animated object must succeed on a Constitution saving throw against the caster's spell save DC or fall unconscious for one minute.
Constructed Nature. An animated object doesn't require air, food, drink, or sleep.
False Appearance. While the animated object remains motionless, it is indistinguishable from a normal object of its type.

Actions

Multiattack. The animated object makes two Slam attacks.
Slam. *Melee Weapon Attack:* +6 to hit, reach 5 ft., one target. *Hit:* 6 (1d4 + 4) bludgeoning damage.

Azizou (Pain Demon)
Small fiend (demon), chaotic evil

Armor Class 15 (natural armor)
Hit Points 17 (5d6)
Speed 30 ft., fly 50 ft.

STR	DEX	CON	INT	WIS	CHA
14 (+2)	15 (+2)	11 (+0)	8 (–1)	10 (+0)	8 (–1)

Skills Deception +3, Stealth +4
Damage Resistances cold, fire, lightning
Damage Immunities poison
Condition Immunities poisoned
Senses darkvision 60 ft., passive Perception 10
Languages Abyssal
Challenge 3 (700 XP)

Magic Resistance. The demon has advantage on saving throws against spells and other magical effects.
Magic Weapons. The demon's weapon attacks are magical.
Innate Spellcasting. The demon's spellcasting ability is Charisma (spell save DC 9). The demon can innately cast the following spells at will, requiring no material components: *detect evil and good, detect thoughts, invisibility.*

Actions

Multiattack. The demon makes one Bite attack and two Claw attacks.
Bite. *Melee Weapon Attack:* +4 to hit, reach 5 ft., one target. *Hit:* 5 (1d6 + 2) piercing damage.
Claws. *Melee Weapon Attack:* +4 to hit, reach 5 ft., one target. *Hit:* 4 (1d4 + 2) slashing damage.

Cipatenhua
Medium humanoid (cipatenhua), chaotic neutral

Armor Class 13 (natural armor)
Hit Points 22 (4d8 + 4)**Speed** 30 ft., swim 30 ft.

STR	DEX	CON	INT	WIS	CHA
15 (+2)	10 (+0)	13 (+1)	9 (–1)	12 (+1)	9 (–1)

Skills Perception +3, Stealth +2, Survival +3**Senses** passive Perception 13
Languages Common, Draconic
Challenge 1/2 (100 XP)

Curse of Itztliteotl. A cipatenhua who is not in contact with water, wet earth, or another wet surface at the start of its turn takes 1d6 necrotic damage.
Hold Breath. The cipatenhua can hold its breath for 15 minutes.
River Predator. The cipatenhua has advantage on Dexterity (Stealth) checks made to hide in coast and swamp terrain.

Actions

Multiattack. The cipatenhua makes two melee attacks, each one with a different weapon.
Bite. *Melee Weapon Attack:* +4 to hit, reach 5 ft., one target. *Hit:* 5 (1d6+2) piercing damage, and the target is grappled (escape DC 12). The cipatenhua has one bite, which can grapple only one target.
Greatclub. *Melee Weapon Attack:* +4 to hit reach 5 ft., one target. *Hit:* 6 (1d8+2) bludgeoning damage.

Cipatenhua Disciple of Tsathogga
Medium humanoid (cipatenhua), chaotic evil

Armor Class 14 (natural armor)
Hit Points 44 (8d8 + 8)**Speed** 30 ft., swim 30 ft.

STR	DEX	CON	INT	WIS	CHA
15 (+2)	10 (+0)	13 (+1)	10 (+0)	12 (+1)	12 (+1)

Skills Perception +3, Stealth +2, Survival +3**Senses** passive Perception 13
Languages Common, Draconic
Challenge 2 (450 XP)

Curse of Itztliteotl. A cipatenhua who is not in contact with water, wet earth, or another wet surface at the start of its turn takes 1d6 necrotic damage.
Hold Breath. The cipatenhua can hold its breath for 15 minutes.
River Predator. The cipatenhua has advantage on Dexterity (Stealth) checks made to hide in coast and swamp terrain.
Spellcaster (cipatenhua form only). The cipatenhua disciple is a 6th-level spellcaster. Its spellcasting ability is Charisma (spell save DC 11, +3 to hit with spell attacks). The cipatenhua disciple has the following warlock spells prepared:

Cantrips (at will): *chill touch, eldritch blast, jinx*[a]
Spells (2 slots): *gaseous form, hex, instill madness*[a], *misty step, spider climb, vampiric touch, witch bolt*[a] See **Appendix C: New Spells**

Actions

Multiattack (cipatenhua form only). The cipatenhua disciple makes one Bite attack and one Greatclub attack.

Bite. *Melee Weapon Attack:* +4 to hit, reach 5 ft., one target. *Hit:* 5 (1d6 + 2) piercing damage, and the target is grappled (escape DC 12). The cipatenhua has one bite, which can grapple only one target.

Greatclub (cipatenhua form only). *Melee Weapon Attack:* +4 to hit, reach 5 ft., one target. *Hit:* 6 (1d8 + 2) bludgeoning damage.

Touch of Madness (recharges after a short of long rest). *Melee Weapon Attack:* +4 to hit, reach 5 ft., one target. *Hit:* 4 (1d4 + 2) bludgeoning damage plus 10 (3d6) psychic damage. If the target is a creature with an Intelligence score of 5 or greater, it must succeed on a DC 11 Wisdom saving throw or become stunned while babbling incoherently. At the end of each of its turns, and each time it takes damage, the target can make another Wisdom saving throw. The target has advantage on the saving throw if it is triggered by damage. On a success, the babbling ends, and the target is no longer stunned.

Change Shape (recharges after a short or long rest). The cipatenhua disciple magically polymorphs into a giant frog and can remain in that form for up to one hour. It can revert to its true form as a bonus action. Its statistics, other than its size, are the same in each form. Any equipment it is wearing or carrying is not transformed. It reverts to its true form if it dies.

CIPATENHUA FROG PRIEST

Medium humanoid (cipatenhua), chaotic evil

Armor Class 13 (natural armor)
Hit Points 66 (12d8 + 12)**Speed** 30 ft., swim 30 ft.

STR	DEX	CON	INT	WIS	CHA
15 (+2)	10 (+0)	13 (+1)	10 (+0)	14 (+2)	10 (+0)

Skills Perception +4, Religion +2, Survival +4**Senses** passive Perception 14
Languages Common, Draconic
Challenge 3 (700 XP)

Curse of Itztliteotl. A cipatenhua who is not in contact with water, wet earth, or another wet surface at the start of its turn takes 1d6 necrotic damage.

Hold Breath. The cipatenhua can hold its breath for 15 minutes.

River Predator. The cipatenhua has advantage on Dexterity (Stealth) checks made to hide in coast and swamp terrain.

Spellcaster (cipatenhua form only). The cipatenhua frog priest is a 6th-level spellcaster. Its spellcasting ability is Wisdom (spell save DC 12, +4 to hit with spell attacks). The cipatenhua disciple has the following cleric spells prepared.
Cantrips (at will): *guidance, mending, sacred flame, spare the dying*
1st level (4 slots): *bloodbath*[a], *inflict wounds, shield of faith*
2nd level (3 slots): *blindness/deafness, hold person, spiritual weapon*
3rd level (3 slots): *bestow curse, flay skin*[aa] See **Appendix C: New Spells**

Actions

Multiattack (cipatenhua form only). The cipatenhua frog priest makes one Bite attack and one Greatclub attack.

Bite. *Melee Weapon Attack:* +4 to hit, reach 5 ft., one target. *Hit:* 5 (1d6 + 2) piercing damage, and the target is grappled (escape DC 12). The cipatenhua frog priest has one bite, which can grapple only one target.

Greatclub (cipatenhua form only). *Melee Weapon Attack:* +4 to hit, reach 5 ft., one target. *Hit:* 6 (1d8 + 2) bludgeoning damage.

Crazed Croak (recharges 5–6). The frog priest emits a disturbing croak. Every humanoid and giant within 30 feet of the frog priest that can hear the croak must succeed on a DC 12 Wisdom saving throw or become disturbed by horrific visions. A creature disturbed by these images cannot concentrate on any task, including casting spells or maintaining spells requiring concentration, and the creature suffers disadvantage on subsequent Charisma, Intelligence, and Wisdom skills checks and saving throws. At the end of each of its turns, the target can attempt another saving throw, albeit at disadvantage. On a success, the visions immediately cease.

Change Shape (recharges after a short or long rest). The frog priest magically polymorphs into a giant frog and can remain in that form for up to one hour. It can revert to its true form as a bonus action. Its statistics, other than its size, are the same in each form. Any equipment it is wearing or carrying is not transformed. It reverts to its true form if it dies.

CIPATENHUA FROG PRINCE

Medium humanoid (cipatenhua), chaotic evil

Armor Class 15 (natural armor)
Hit Points 104 (16d8 + 32)
Speed 30 ft., swim 30 ft.

STR	DEX	CON	INT	WIS	CHA
15 (+2)	10 (+0)	14 (+2)	12 (+1)	12 (+1)	12 (+1)

Skills Athletics +4, Perception +3, Survival +3**Condition Immunities** charmed, frightened
Senses passive Perception 13
Languages Common, Draconic
Challenge 4 (1,100 XP)

Curse of Itztliteotl. A cipatenhua who is not in contact with water, wet earth, or another wet surface at the start of its turn takes 1d6 necrotic damage.

Fanatical Devotion. The frog prince cannot be charmed or frightened.

Hold Breath. The cipatenhua can hold its breath for 15 minutes.

River Predator. The cipatenhua has advantage on Dexterity (Stealth) checks made to hide in coast and swamp terrain.

Actions

Multiattack (cipatenhua form only). The cipatenhua frog prince makes one Bite attack and one Greatclub attack.

Bite. *Melee Weapon Attack:* +4 to hit, reach 5 ft., one target. *Hit:* 5 (1d6 + 2) piercing damage, and the target is grappled (escape DC 12). The cipatenhua frog prince has one bite, which can grapple only one target.

Greatclub (cipatenhua form only). *Melee Weapon Attack:* +4 to hit, reach 5 ft., one target. *Hit:* 6 (1d8 + 2) bludgeoning damage.

Blood in the Water. When the cipatenhua prince hits a creature with a melee attack, the creature takes an extra 1d8 damage if it is below its hit point maximum. The cipatenhua prince can deal this extra damage only once per turn.

Change Shape (recharges after a short or long rest). The cipatenhua prince magically polymorphs into a giant frog and can remain in that form for up to one hour. It can revert to its true form as a bonus action. Its statistics, other than its size, are the same in each form. Any equipment it is wearing or carrying is not transformed. It reverts to its true form if it dies.

Tsathogga's Cursed Touch (recharges after a short or long rest). *Melee Weapon Attack:* +4 to hit, reach 5 ft., one target. *Hit:* 4 (1d4 + 2) bludgeoning damage plus 16 (3d10) necrotic damage. If the target is a creature other than a construct or an undead, it must succeed on a DC 12 Constitution saving throw or be cursed by Tsathogga. The cursed target's hit point maximum is reduced by an amount equal to the necrotic damage taken. The reduction lasts until the target finishes a long rest. If the curse reduces the target's hit point maximum to 0, the target dies, and its body turns to festering pustules of rancid flesh.

DEMONIC MIST

Medium fiend (demon), chaotic evil

Armor Class 16 (natural armor)
Hit Points 85 (10d8 + 40)
Speed fly 50 ft.

STR	DEX	CON	INT	WIS	CHA
6 (+2)	18 (+4)	18 (+4)	8 (–1)	13 (+1)	16 (+3)

Saving Throws Dex +6, Con +6
Skills Perception +3, Stealth +6
Damage Resistances acid, fire, cold; bludgeoning, piercing, and slashing from nonmagical attacks
Damage Immunities poison
Condition Immunities poisoned
Senses darkvision 60 ft., passive Perception 13
Languages Abyssal, Telepathy 120 ft.
Challenge 4 (1,100 XP)

Incorporeal Movement. The demonic mist can move through other creatures and objects as if they were difficult terrain. It takes 5 (1d10) force damage if it ends its turn inside an object.
Innate Spellcasting. A demonic mist's spellcasting ability is Charisma (spell save DC 13, +5 to hit with spell attacks), and requires no material components for the following spells:
At will: *detect magic*
3/day each: *ray of enfeeblement, vampiric touch*
1/day each: *confusion, fear*
Vulnerability to Wind. The demonic mist has disadvantage on saving throws against wind and wind-like effects (*gust of wind,* etc.).

Actions

Demonic Touch. *Melee Weapon Attack:* +6 to hit, reach 5 ft., one target. *Hit:* 25 (6d6 + 4) necrotic damage.
***Psychic Crush* (recharge 5–6).** The demonic mist attempts to crush the mind of a single creature it can see within 30 feet. The target must make a successful DC 15 Wisdom saving throw or take 14 (4d6) psychic damage and be frightened for one minute.

GOLEM, WOOD

Medium construct, unaligned

Armor Class 14 (natural armor)
Hit Points 52 (8d8 + 16)
Speed 20 ft.

STR	DEX	CON	INT	WIS	CHA
18 (+4)	10 (+0)	15 (+2)	3 (–4)	10 (+0)	1 (–5)

Damage Vulnerabilities fire
Damage Resistances bludgeoning, piercing, and slashing from nonmagical attacks not made with adamantine
Damage Immunities poison, psychic
Condition Immunities charmed, exhaustion, frightened, paralyzed, petrified, poisoned
Senses darkvision 60 ft., passive Perception 10
Languages understands the languages of its creator but can't speak
Challenge 3 (700 XP)

Immutable Form. The golem is immune to any spell or effect that would alter its form.
Magic Resistance. The wood golem has advantage on saving throws against spells and other magical effects.

Actions

Multiattack. The wood golem makes two Slam attacks.
Slam. *Melee Weapon Attack:* +6 to hit, reach 5 ft., one target. *Hit:* 8 (1d8 + 4) bludgeoning damage.
The golem, wood can be found in *Creature Codex* by **Kobold Press**.

HELLCAT

Tiny aberration, neutral evil

Armor Class 14 (natural armor)
Hit Points 44 (8d4 + 24)
Speed 40 ft., climb 30 ft.

STR	DEX	CON	INT	WIS	CHA
3 (–4)	15 (+2)	16 (+3)	11 (+0)	15 (+2)	18 (+4)

Saving Throws Int +2, Wis +4
Skills Perception +4, Stealth +4
Senses darkvision 60 ft., passive Perception 14
Languages understands Common but can't speak; telepathy 60 ft.
Challenge 2 (450 XP)

Death Sense. The hellcat can sense the exact location of any humanoid within 120 feet that has fewer than half its hit points.
False Appearance. Unless it is using its Death Gaze ability, the hellcat is indistinguishable from a normal housecat.
Magic Resistance. The hellcat has advantage on saving throws against spells and other magical effects.

Actions

Multiattack. The hellcat makes one Bite attack and one Claw attack.
Bite. *Melee Weapon Attack:* +4 to hit, reach 5 ft., one target. *Hit:* 4 (1d4 + 2) piercing damage.
Claws. *Melee Weapon Attack:* +4 to hit, reach 5 ft., one target. *Hit:* 9 (2d6 + 2) slashing damage.
***Death Gaze* (recharge 5–6).** One target within 30 feet of the hellcat that it can see must make a DC 14 Constitution saving throw. On a failed saving throw, the target takes 27 (6d8) necrotic damage. If the creature drops to 0 hit points from this damage, it dies, and can be restored to life only by means of a *true resurrection* or *wish* spell.

OOZE, MUDBOG

Large ooze, unaligned

Armor Class 9
Hit Points 51 (6d10 + 18)
Speed 10 ft., swim 10 ft.

STR	DEX	CON	INT	WIS	CHA
20 (+5)	8 (–1)	17 (+3)	1 (–5)	10 (+0)	3 (–4)

Skills Stealth +1
Senses blindsight 60 ft. (blind beyond this radius), passive Perception 10
Damage Resistances fire
Damage Immunities acid, psychic
Condition Immunities blinded, charmed, deafened, exhaustion, frightened, prone
Languages —
Challenge 2 (450 XP)

Acid. A mudbog secretes a digestive acid that quickly dissolves organic material, but not metal or stone. A creature that attacks the mudbog takes 3 (1d6) acid damage. Any wood or other organic material that touches the mudbog is pitted. Wooden weapons suffer a cumulative

−1 penalty to damage rolls made with it unless it is magical. When this penalty reaches −5, the weapon is destroyed.

Amorphous. The ooze can move through a space as narrow as one inch wide without squeezing.

False Appearance. The mudbog, while not moving, is indistinguishable from a muddy puddle.

Actions

Engulf. The mudbog moves up to its speed. While doing so, it can enter Medium or smaller creatures' spaces. Whenever the mudbog enters a creature's space, the creature must make a DC 13 Dexterity saving throw. On a failed save, the creature is engulfed and the mudbog enters the creature's space. The creature takes 10 (3d6) acid damage. The engulfed creature can't breathe, is restrained, and takes 21 (6d6) acid damage at the start of each of the ooze's turns. When the mudbog moves, the engulfed creature moves with it.

An engulfed creature can try to escape by taking an action to make a DC14 Strength (Athletics) check. On a success, the creature escapes and enters a space of its choice within five feet of the ooze.

On a successful save, the creature can choose to be pushed five feet back or to the side of the mudbog. A creature that chooses not to be pushed suffers the consequences of a failed saving throw.

Bite. *Melee Weapon Attack:* +3 to hit, reach 0 ft., one target. *Hit:* 11 (3d6−1) piercing damage, and the target must succeed on a DC 12 Constitution saving throw or be poisoned for one hour.

SLOTH VIPER

Large monstrosity, neutral

Armor Class 16 (natural armor)
Hit Points 38 (7d10)
Speed 30 ft., climb 30 ft., swim 30 ft.

STR	DEX	CON	INT	WIS	CHA
13 (+1)	16 (+3)	11 (+0)	2 (−4)	12 (+1)	2 (−4)

Skills Perception +3, Stealth +5
Senses darkvision 60 ft., passive Perception 13
Languages —
Challenge 2 (450 XP)

Actions

Bite. *Melee Weapon Attack:* +5 to hit, reach 5 ft., one target. *Hit:* 7 (1d8 + 3) piercing damage, and the target must succeed on a DC 13 Constitution saving throw. On a failed saving throw, the target takes 14 (4d6) poison damage and the target is poisoned for one minute. On a successful saving throw, the target takes half damage and is not poisoned.

While the target is poisoned, its speed is halved, it can't use reactions, and it can take only one action or one bonus action on each of its turns, and regardless of abilities or magic items, it can't make more than one melee or ranged attack during its turn. If the creature attempts to cast a spell with a casting time of 1 action, roll a d20. On an 11 or higher, the spell does not take effect until the creature's next turn, and the creature must use its action on that turn to complete the spell. If it cannot, the spell is wasted.

SWARM OF POISONOUS FROGS

Medium swarm of Tiny beasts, unaligned

Armor Class 13 (natural armor)
Hit Points 59 (17d8 − 17)
Speed 20 ft., swim 20 ft.

STR	DEX	CON	INT	WIS	CHA
1 (−5)	13 (+1)	8 (−1)	1 (−5)	8 (−1)	3 (−4)

Skills Perception +1, Stealth +3
Damage Immunities poison
Condition Immunities poisoned
Senses passive Perception 11
Languages –
Challenge 1 (200 XP)

Amphibious. The swarm can breathe air and water

Keen Smell. The swarm has advantage on Wisdom (Perception) checks that rely on smell.

Standing Leap. The swarm's long jump is up to 10 feet and its high jump is up to five feet, with or without a running start.

Swarm. The swarm can occupy another creature's space and vice versa, and the swarm can move through any opening large enough for a poisonous frog. The swarm can't regain hit points or gain temporary hit points.

Actions

Bite. *Melee Weapon Attack:* +3 to hit, reach 0 ft., one target. *Hit:* 9 (3d6 − 1) piercing damage, and the target must succeed on a DC 12 Constitution saving throw or be poisoned for one hour.

T'SHANN

Small aberration, neutral

Armor Class 8 (natural armor)
Hit Points 32 (5d6 + 15)
Speed 10 ft., burrow 10 ft.

STR	DEX	CON	INT	WIS	CHA
10 (+0)	4 (−3)	16 (+3)	2 (−4)	10 (+0)	12 (+1)

Senses blindsight 60 ft. (blind beyond this radius), passive Perception 10
Languages —
Challenge 1 (200 XP)

Acidic Secretion. A creature who touches the t'shann takes 5 (2d4) acid damage. Any nonmagical weapon made of metal or wood that hits the t'shann corrodes. After dealing damage, the weapon takes a permanent and cumulative −1 penalty to damage rolls. If its penalty drops to −5, the weapon is destroyed. Nonmagical ammunition made of metal or wood that hits the t'shann is destroyed after dealing damage.

In addition, nonmagical armor worn by the target of any of the t'shann's attacks is partly dissolved and takes a permanent and cumulative −1 penalty to the AC it offers. The armor is destroyed if the penalty reduces its AC to 10.

Alien Thoughts. When a creature enters or starts its turn within 30 feet of the t'shann, the creature must make a DC 13 Wisdom saving throw, unless the t'shann is incapacitated. On a failed saving throw, the creature can't take reactions until the start of its next turn and rolls a d8 to determine what it does during that turn. On a 1–4, the creature does nothing. On a 5 or 6, the creature takes no action but uses all its movement to move in a random direction. On a 7 or 8, the creature makes one melee attack against a random creature, or it does nothing if no creature is within reach.

Actions

Slam. *Melee Weapon Attack:* +2 to hit, reach 5 ft., one target. *Hit:* 2 (1d4) bludgeoning damage plus 5 (2d4) acid damage.

Spew Acid. *Ranged Weapon Attack:* +2 to hit, range 10 ft., one target. *Hit:* 5 (2d4) acid damage.

TSATHAR

Medium monstrosity (aquatic), chaotic evil

Armor Class 13 (natural armor)
Hit Points 16 (3d8 + 3)
Speed 30 ft., swim 30 ft.

STR	DEX	CON	INT	WIS	CHA
13 (+1)	14 (+2)	12 (+1)	12 (+1)	12 (+1)	10 (+0)

Skills Stealth +4
Senses darkvision 60 ft., passive Perception 11
Languages Abyssal, Tsathar
Challenge 1/2 (100 XP)

Amphibious. The tsathar can breathe air and water.

Keen Smell. The tsathar has advantage on Wisdom (Perception) checks that rely on smell.

Slimy. Tsathar continuously cover themselves with muck and slime. Creatures attempting to grapple a tsathar do so with disadvantage.

Standing Leap. The tsathar's long jump is up to 20 feet and its high jump is up to 10 feet, with or without a running start.

Actions

Multiattack. The tsathar makes one Bite attack and one Claw attack, or one Bite attack and one Spear attack.

Bite. *Melee Weapon Attack:* +3 to hit, reach 5 ft., one target. *Hit:* 3 (1d4 + 1) piercing damage.

Claws. *Melee Weapon Attack:* +3 to hit, reach 5 ft., one target. *Hit:* 3 (1d4 + 1) slashing damage, and the target must succeed on a DC 13 Constitution saving throw or become the living host to a tsathar egg, which over the course of the egg maturing, migrates to the chest cavity of the host. The host creature must make another DC 13 Constitution saving throw after 24 hours of the egg having been implanted. A failed saving throw results in the host becoming violently ill, followed by a deep coma-like state that lasts 2d6 + 2 days. At the end of each day, the host can attempt another saving throw, with a success indicating that its body has managed to destroy the egg through normal immune response. At the end of the incubation period, the host awakes to excruciating pain as the young tsathar, freed from its egg, tears its way out of the host, who is reduced to 0 hit points in the process. A DC 16 Wisdom (Medicine) check can be attempted to surgically extract an egg from the host. A *lesser restoration* spell also cures the condition and purges the host of the egg.

Spear. *Melee Weapon Attack:* +3 to hit, reach 5 ft. or 20/60 ft., one target. *Hit:* 4 (1d6 + 1) piercing damage, or 5 (1d8 + 1) piercing damage if used with two hands to make the melee attack.

Appendix B: New Items and Magic

The following items and magic are found in this adventure:

New Weapons

Itztopilli. This axe has a wooden haft with a bronze head fitted into a groove built into the haft. The head is long and narrow, and its cutting surface is only slightly wider than the axe's flat back. The itztopilli's versatile design allows you to hack into flesh as well as chop wood with remarkable accuracy and comparable ease. Indeed, most woodworkers incorporate the weapon into a standard set of carpenter's tools. If you are proficient with the itztopilli, and you made an attack roll with the weapon within the last 24 hours, you also gain proficiency with carpenter's tools.

Equipment

Xochitl. A creature that drinks this vial of vanilla-flavored liquid suffers disadvantage on saving throws against being put to sleep by magic for one hour. Alternatively, a creature that drinks xochitl less than one hour before beginning a long rest falls into a deep slumber. A creature who normally needs eight hours of sleep awakens refreshed after four hours of sleep, as if it had completed its long rest.

Magic Items

Arrow of Flesh Finding

Weapon (arrow), uncommon

This arrow is a magic weapon with the unusual ability to avoid striking inanimate objects in its path. When you make a ranged attack roll with the arrow, the target of your ranged attack does not gain any AC bonus from half-cover or three-quarters cover granted by an inanimate object. You have advantage on your ranged attack roll with the arrow if the target is wearing armor or holding a shield. If the target's body is made of flesh, the arrow deals an extra 3d10 piercing damage on a successful hit. Once an *arrow of flesh finding* hits a target, it becomes a nonmagical arrow.

Cuacalalatli of the Beast

Wondrous item, rarity varies (requires attunement)

These wooden helmets are shaped into the likenesses of various beast heads. The protective device fits over your head, covering the top and back of your skull as well as your jawline. While wearing this helmet, you gain its abilities. The type of beast associated with the helmet determines its specific properties.

Frog (uncommon): You feel equally at home fighting in water as you do on dry land. You can hold your breath for 15 minutes, and you do not have disadvantage when making a melee weapon attack while underwater.

War Paint

Wondrous item, rarity varies

Typically stored in clay jars two inches in diameter, each container holds 1d3 applications of viscous pigments made from dyes and other colorful components. Each jar contains one color of paint, and its contents weigh one-half pound. As an action, one dose of war paint can be rubbed onto the skin. The pigment covers roughly six square inches of skin. A creature can wear no more than three different colors of paint at a time, and you cannot simultaneously apply the effects of more than one color of *war paint* to the same weapon. Any attempt to apply more than three colors of war paint fails. Each application of paint lasts for 10 minutes regardless of color. The *war paint's* color determines its effects.

Purple (uncommon): You are a whirlwind in combat. When a creature you can see within reach takes damage from a melee attack during another creature's turn, you can use your reaction to make a melee attack against the creature that took the hit.

Table C–1: Tehuatl Weapons

Weapon	Cost	Damage	Weight	Properties	Equivalent
Simple Melee Weapons					
Itztopilli	4 gp	1d6 slashing	2 lbs.	Light, special, thrown (range 20/60)	Handaxe

Appendix C: New Spells

The following spells are found in this adventure:

Bloodbath

1st-level transmutation
Casting Time: 1 action
Range: 30 feet
Components: V, S, M (a drop of your own blood)
Duration: Instantaneous

You create 10 gallons of blood within range in an open container. Alternatively, the blood splashes onto all creatures and objects in a 30-foot cube within range. The blood extinguishes exposed flames in the area and is identical in composition to your own blood. Each creature within the area must succeed on a Wisdom saving throw or drop whatever it is holding and be disgusted. Until the end of your next turn, the disgusted creature cannot willingly move closer to you and averts its eyes from you, preventing it from seeing you. Creatures that cannot be frightened are still doused in blood but are otherwise not affected by this spell.

Flay Skin

3rd-level transmutation
Casting Time: 1 action
Range: 30 feet
Components: V, S, M (an obsidian chip)
Duration: Instantaneous

Choose a creature other than an undead or construct you can see within range. The target must succeed on a Constitution saving throw or take 8d6 slashing damage and have portions of its skin flayed from its body. On a successful save, the creature takes half as much damage and its skin is not flayed. Creatures with flayed skin that have natural armor take a −2 penalty to AC. In addition, these creatures become vulnerable to acid, cold, fire, and lightning damage. A creature can take an action to repair the flayed skin with a successful Wisdom (Medicine) check against your spell save DC. The skin also mends itself if the target receives magical healing.

Instill Madness

3rd-level enchantment
Casting Time: 1 action
Range: 120 feet
Components: V, S
Duration: Concentration, up to 1 minute

One humanoid of your choice that you can see within range must succeed on a Wisdom saving throw or succumb to madness for the duration. While in the throes of madness, the target is no longer an ally, companion, or non-hostile creature toward any another creature for the purpose of determining whether ongoing or new spells and effects affect the target. While mad, the target cannot take bonus actions or reactions and can only move or take the Attack or Dash actions. It cannot use or activate magic items, interact with objects it is not already holding, or use any class features unless those features aid its movement or attacks. The madness instantly breaks its concentration and also causes the target to have disadvantage on Charisma, Intelligence, and Wisdom checks and saving throws, including those to end this spell.

The target is free to decide whether to move, Attack, or Dash, but when it does so, it acts randomly. If the target moves or takes the Dash action, it uses all its movement to move in a random direction until it completes its movement or another creature, obstacle, or obviously deadly hazard blocks its path. To determine the direction, roll a d8 and assign a direction to each die face. The target can attack only with natural weapons or any weapon it held when it succumbed to its madness. If the target makes a melee attack, it attacks a random creature within its reach. If the target makes a ranged attack, it targets a random creature it can see within range. The target continues to attack random creatures until another creature it can see hits it with an attack. The target then attacks that creature until the spell ends. If more than one creature hits the target, the target randomly determines which creature it attacks.

At the end of each of its turns, an affected target can make a Wisdom saving throw. If it succeeds, this effect ends for that target.

Jinx

Divination cantrip
Casting Time: 1 action
Range: 30 feet
Components: V, S
Duration: 1 minute

A creature of your choice that you can see within range receives an ominous feeling that something bad is about to happen. The target must succeed on a Wisdom saving throw or be jinxed. On a successful Wisdom saving throw, the target is not affected, and you cannot use this cantrip against it again for 24 hours. Whenever the target rolls a 1 on any d20 roll, including when the target rolls two dice for advantage or disadvantage, the target's turn ends immediately after resolving the outcome from that die roll, if the die roll took place during the target's turn. Regardless of when the die roll occurred, the target cannot take any reactions until the beginning of its next turn. The target then has disadvantage on attack rolls, saving throws, and ability checks made until the end of its next turn when the spell ends for that target. A target can be affected by only one *jinx* spell at a time. If you or another creature casts this spell on a target already affected by this spell, the first *jinx* spell immediately ends.

You can target additional creatures when you reach higher levels: two creatures at 5th level, three creatures at 11th level, and four creatures at 17th level.

www.ingramcontent.com/pod-product-compliance
Lightning Source LLC
Chambersburg PA
CBHW041204100726
47911CB00016B/852